LUCID

ERIKA HARKEN

LUCID

Cover Illustrator: Erika Harken
www.erikaharken.com

Title Page Image by Redd on Unsplash
Used in accordance with the irrevocable, nonexclusive, worldwide copyright license that permits free use for commercial purposes.

ISBN-13: 978-1-7376640-0-0
Library of Congress Control Number: 2022911965

This is a work of fiction. Names, characters, places, incidents, companies or brands are products of the author's imagination and/or used fictitiously.

First Edition: October 2022
Printed in the United States of America

VERUM FICTA PRESS
An imprint of Isaiah Publishing Co.

Davison, Michigan.

Contents

LUCID

PARTNERS | Anna

I dreaded Reforming Literature as I walked into class early that morning. A few students were already seated while I moved toward my desk in the middle of the room, relieved to see the one in front of mine was still empty. After sitting down, I took out a notebook and pencil from my backpack and stared at the whiteboard—hoping the freak that sat in front of me wouldn't show up.

How much does he care about school, anyway?

My gaze shifted to the door a few minutes later when other students poured in, but none of them were *him*—Adam Avery.

After the bell rang, I finally relaxed while our teacher, Mr. Emery, greeted us. He had assigned partners last class for our final project, and now explained that each group had to pick an autobiography to break down into a presentation and essay, which would be worth twenty-five percent of our grade. While Mr. Emery passed out the rubric and answered questions, the perfect book instantly popped into my head: *Spiraled Life* by Allison Stormer.

For a moment, I wondered if I should discuss it with Adam. But since he hadn't shown up, I ultimately decided it didn't matter.

I'll be doing most of the work anyway, so if he doesn't like the book—tough.

I pushed in my earbuds and started writing the outline, becoming lost in my own world of song and focus for a while until—

"Hey, sorry."

I blinked as I laid eyes on Adam Avery, who had suddenly appeared at his desk like a ghost. I ripped my earbuds out as I stared at his semi-apologetic expression.

"Sorry?"

"Yeah—*obviously* I'm late. Didn't mean to be."

My nose wrinkled as I glanced at his lengthy black hair, which had light brown roots and hung untamed around his soft-angled face. Adam wore his typical band t-shirt and ripped jeans, as well as a studded belt and oversized sneakers. I usually couldn't help imagining him groomed and wearing better clothes, but despite how much being his assigned partner disturbed me, there wasn't much I actually knew about him.

Why does he have to be so weird and look that way? Doesn't he know what everyone thinks?

"Don't worry," I replied quickly. "I already chose a book. It's called Spiraled Life by Allison Stormer."

"Cool. I guess I'm out of here, then."

"Wait—*you're leaving?* You just got here!"

"Relax! I'm going to the library to get the book, okay?"

Adam rolled his eyes as he stood up, and I frowned while he got permission from Mr. Emery and left.

Don't tell me to relax! Why is he so rude?

I sighed heavily as I looked at his empty desk, certain that he wasn't thrilled to have me as a partner, either.

* * * * * *

Two days later, I sat in the middle of the cafeteria with my best friend Natalie. Her shoulder-length blonde hair almost blended with her pale skin, and we'd first met in the sixth grade, where we bonded through horses and boy bands. While we talked about one of our favorite TV shows, I suddenly noticed Adam at the end of the lunch line across the room. Instinctively, I felt the impulse to ignore him, but he *hadn't* come back to class after going to the library on Tuesday—nor had he been in Reform Lit that morning.

"What is it with him?" I snapped, breaking our conversation.

"Who?" Natalie asked curiously.

"Adam! He's been ditching class, but now he's right *there!*"

Natalie's gaze followed the direction I pointed in, her mouth curving into a frown.

"He might have skipped first period with Luna," she suggested plainly. "I think they're dating."

I furrowed my brow and looked at Adam again, this time spotting Luna Caldwell standing on the other side of him. Natalie and I had a class with her sophomore year, and I remembered her being quiet and slightly awkward back then. But ever since joining Adam's crowd, she no longer dressed normally, and dyed her hair different colors like most of them did.

"I bet they are," I replied. "Too bad Luna wanted to be like him. Do you think they'll go to prom?"

Natalie shrugged and took a bite of her sandwich.

"I doubt Adam cares about it, but she probably does. Has... anyone asked yet?"

I groaned and shook my head.

"No, but Jake *still* can't ask one of his friends. I'm saving that as a last resort."

"Okay—fine."

Jake was Natalie's boyfriend, and their *amazing* idea to find me a date had only made me feel pathetic.

My gaze dropped to my chocolate pudding as I thought about how annoying it was that Adam had ditched class twice. But even worse than that—I felt jealous of him, too. Prom was nothing short of a joke to him... yet *he* could have a legitimate date easily if he wanted.

Once lunch ended, I said goodbye to Natalie and went to class, sulking.

Why hasn't God given me a prom date yet? Or even better—a boyfriend? Why does Adam have to get what I want?

I felt tortured by those thoughts for the rest of the day, and when school ended a few hours later, I walked across the senior parking lot in a bitter mood. The flurry of happy voices and laughter didn't help, and I had almost reached my car before an irritating sound stopped me.

"Hey, Anna!"

I turned, seeing Adam jogging toward me. When he stopped a few feet away, he slid his backpack off his shoulder.

"I have notes on Spiraled Life," he said quickly. "Look them over and use what you want."

I crossed my arms and frowned as he dug through his bag and pulled out a few sheets of paper.

"Why weren't you in class?" I asked heatedly. "This project is *extremely* important—it's worth twenty-five percent of our grade."

Adam shrugged, his expression defensive.

"I had to deal with something. I'll be there next week."

I took the notes from his hand and made a skeptical noise.

"What's more important than class? Do I have to do all the work by myself?"

"No, you don't," he snapped. "I didn't come back from the library because I wanted to focus and write good notes, which I just gave you. And my girlfriend was upset this morning, so I had to be there for her."

I rolled my eyes, even though his excuses seemed reasonable.

"Judge me all you want, but I'm not stupid. I know what you and your friends think of me, and it doesn't mean a damn thing."

Adam spit on the ground near my shoe, causing me to jump backward. I stood rigid in shock while he stalked off, watching him until he disappeared in the crowd.

· · · · · ·

"Should I ask for a new partner?"

I sounded desperate as I leaned against the kitchen counter that evening while my mom unpacked our groceries. Though we shared the same dark brown hair and gray eyes, she stood a few inches shorter than me.

"You could," she replied. "But I think you should give it more time. Remember Pastor Dave preaching about being a light to the world? Maybe you should be one to Adam."

I laughed, then groaned.

"But he's so horrible. I'm sure he thinks I'm an idiot for being a Christian, too."

"Well, I bet if he really got to know you, he might see things a little differently."

"So, spitting on my feet in the parking lot doesn't matter?"

"You said it was near your foot."

"Same thing, basically."

"If you want a new partner, then ask your teacher, but I think you shouldn't give up so soon."

I frowned at my mom, realizing that no matter what I said, she wasn't going to understand and had nothing helpful to say. Without a word, I left the kitchen and went upstairs, where I laid on my bed and squeezed my eyes shut.

Why can't she understand how impossible this is? I don't even know how I'm going to speak another word to him, much less be a light...

I sat up slowly and glanced at my backpack, which I'd thrown against the wall earlier. Adam's notes were inside, and though I didn't want to touch them again, curiosity soon got the better of me. I climbed off my bed and fished out the notes, scanning his clean handwriting before I focused more intensely. A few quotes he'd written down were highlighted in my own copy of *Spiraled Life*, and his thoughts in the margins were somewhat impressive.

Maybe he does care about this project, even if he doesn't have any manners...

I put Adam's notes back and turned toward my nightstand, where I grabbed my sketch pad and a French magazine called *Coutures* from the top drawer. After sitting cross-legged on my bed, I opened the magazine to the featured spread, which showed dresses from last year's fall fashion show by Estelle Bisset, a renowned designer of luxury evening gowns. My favorite design was a champagne colored dress with a delicately beaded bodice, thin shoulder strap, and a wide, ruffled skirt parted by a slit on one side. It had inspired my latest sketch, and I glanced at the torso mannequin surrounded by fabric and tulle in the corner of my purple room, which had the beginnings of my own prom dress on it.

I tore out the picture of Estelle's dress and slipped it into the memo board on the wall next to the mannequin. Although I would never try to make something like that—*yet*—I could, at least, be brave enough to finish the simple dress pattern I'd bought and started.

The pattern package, which laid on the floor at the foot of the mannequin, showed a strapless dress with an A-line skirt that rose above the knee but trailed down to the floor in the back. The dress pictured was black, but I'd chosen a dark raspberry fabric instead, and decided to add a layer of tulle on top of the skirt for more dimension.

I knelt on the floor and played music from my phone, eager to let the stress of the day disappear as I began cutting fabric.

LUCID | Adam

My cell read 7:51 a.m. while I puffed on a short cig in my black '90s Thunderbird. I leaned back in the driver's seat, the window slightly rolled down while I sat alone in the school parking lot. If I was late or skipped Reform Lit again, my prissy project partner would finally explode.

Wonder how she'll act today, after getting called on her bull...

The whole year I'd sat in front of her, we'd never talked much, but her Christian faith and above ground social status had been crystal clear. Anna also liked looking polished, and always wore pretty makeup, trendy clothes, and kept her long brown hair straight and shiny.

I grinned, imagining her waking up each morning with messy hair and a plain face.

Bet she hates looking in the mirror until she's perfect again... pathetic...

I snuffed my cig out in an empty fast food cup and grabbed my backpack from the passenger seat, slinging it over my shoulder as I walked toward Gainesville High. The first bell hadn't rung yet when I stepped inside, but I took my time anyway as I walked to Emery's class. Once I got there—and *on time*—I thought Anna would just ignore me, but as I sat down at my desk, she looked up and... *smiled*.

"Hi, Adam."

I blinked, my brow furrowing as I stared at her. Anna's smile tightened and she looked away quickly—as if she already regretted being nice to me.

"Your notes were good and I'll work them into my outline. If you want to make the presentation, I'll do the essay."

She talked fast, but I noticed her effort to sound friendly.

"Yeah, sure."

"Great. Thanks."

Her gaze dropped to her notebook as her cheeks turned pink, and I turned around, unable to figure out why she was acting mostly normal.

When the bell rang a few minutes later, Emery reminded us about the field trip next class to see a new Hemingway exhibit, and said the class periods after that would be work days for the final project. Before I got started, I opened my notebook and wrote down some lyrics that were stuck in my head that morning. While I silently mouthed them and tried to imagine the perfect melody, a tap on my shoulder broke my focus. Turning sideways, I met Anna's curious gaze.

"So… do you like the book?"

I blinked, raising a brow. "I guess. Wasn't terrible."

"Good. I thought you'd find it interesting."

"Why?"

"Well, Stormer is… or was… very rebellious."

"Oh. Is that my label?"

Anna raised a brow. "No—what's *mine?*"

"Chill, I'm kidding."

She glared for half a second before her expression relaxed.

"I know Luna Caldwell," she said.

"Yeah? How?"

"We had class together sophomore year. I thought she was nice."

"She's cool. She's my girlfriend."

"Oh—I've seen you guys around, but I wasn't sure."

"She's a lot cooler than you."

Anna's eyes widened with insult, and I faked a yawn as I turned around, her incredibly low sense of humor fun to annoy. I worked on the lyrics for a while longer before I took *Spiraled Life* out of my backpack and started working on a presentation outline. When class ended an hour later, I left without talking to Anna, and found Luna waiting next to my locker. Her short purple hair hung loose around her face, and she wore a black hoodie and ripped jeans.

"Hey, what's up?" she asked.

I shrugged, twisting the com on my locker.

"Anna was weird today."

"You mean Anna Holbach?"

"Yeah—she didn't act like I was made of vomit."

"She still hates you," Luna replied bitterly, unconvinced. "She just wants to get along for a good grade."

"Or maybe the dose of reality she got in the parking lot set her straight."

"Doubt it—she's a terrible person."

I stuffed my math book in my backpack while Luna made a gagging sound, and I held her hand while we walked to our next class.

"She said you had class together sophomore year," I said. "What was that like?"

Luna shrugged, frowning.

"She told me you were nice."

"Really?" Luna said, her nose wrinkling. "I think it was American History, but I don't remember talking to her. She never seemed nice to me. It sucks that you're stuck with her."

Luna squeezed my hand, and I shook my head.

"Don't worry about it," I replied. "I can handle the next five weeks until graduation."

"And then she'll be gone forever," Luna remarked, smiling. "Ready for the show tomorrow night?"

I nodded stiffly, feeling a stab of anxiety.

"Definitely."

● ● ● ● ● ●

The hazy lights around the stage blurred out the crowd on open mic night at Joe's Corner tavern. My band was the last to play, and while me, Nate, and Dex adjusted our equipment on stage, I almost regretted telling them I wanted to sing *Lucid*. I'd written the song a few months ago—and even though singing wasn't my role or even a great skill—some insane part of me wanted to try it.

When we finished prepping, Dex stood beside me with his electric guitar in front of the mic, and Nate sat in the drum set behind us.

"In case you're living under a rock, we're Rebel Riot," he teased coolly into the microphone. "I'm Dex, and this is Adam and Nate. We're getting the hell out of here and going to California soon. If our music sucks—you're wrong."

The crowd of forty-some people laughed, and Nate kicked off our first song with a short drum solo. Dex started singing after, and I used mostly muscle memory to play the right notes while my anxiety surged. Even though I knew the words and chords to *Lucid* perfectly, I'd never sang in front of people, and not screwing up seemed impossible. I stared at my guitar through the first two songs as I focused on staying calm, but before I felt even close to ready, it was my turn to sing.

"Our last song—*Lucid*—was written by Adam," Dex said, slapping me on the back. "And he found the guts to sing it for you tonight. All hail the song virgin!"

Laughter filled the room again as I shot Dex a dirty look, and he smirked while stepping back from the mic. My knees felt weak when I walked in front of it, slightly comforted by the shadows that hid Luna and everyone else in the audience. For a second, I wondered if I needed to say anything, but Dex immediately started the opening riff.

This is it! Do it for California.

Nate joined Dex with a steady drum beat, and I sang after the ten second intro.

Hey I'm sleeping,
Sleeping with you, just as time goes and passes us by.
When will we wake up?
Can we see it, see the light of day again?
Oh my love, if you were true,
I could have never dreamed of someone new.

Here I go, I should know,
That when I'm awake, I won't dream,
but I'll cry and scream.
Yeah I won't dream, but I'll cry and scream.

Hey I'm sleeping,
Sleeping with you, just as love goes and passes us by.
Why did I believe I had to try so hard?
Oh my love, if you were right,
I know I never would have had to fight.

My anxiety melted into an incredible high while I channeled every ounce of stress into the guitar strings. I kept my eyes squeezed shut as my husky voice easily filled the room.

Here I go, I should know,
That when I'm awake,
I won't dream, but I'll cry and scream.
Yeah I won't dream, but I'll cry and scream.

Hey, I'm lucid, with eyes wide open,

But you are fast asleep and gone,
Here's to you, it won't be long,
Until I live in the light of day.

Here I go, now I know,
That when I'm awake,
I won't cry, or scream, just dream.
Yeah I won't cry, or scream, just dream.
Yeah I won't cry, or scream, just dream.

The whole song lasted less than four minutes, but my shirt was drenched in sweat when it ended. Dex stood close to me as the crowd whistled and roared, and Nate appeared on my other side, saluting everyone with a rock n' roll hand gesture. We soaked up the glory for several minutes until we left the stage, exiting the hot tavern through a door leading into the back parking lot. The three of us faced each other under a grimy yellow light, shouting in excitement as we jumped around.

"Where's my money?" Dex asked, looking at Nate.

He was the tallest of us by a few inches, and the sides of his head were buzzed short, but the top had long spiked pieces. I furrowed my brow as I glanced from him to Nate, unsure of what money he was talking about.

"Dammit Adam," Nate said, digging in his pocket. "I have to give Dex ten bucks now because you didn't screw up or get booed."

Nate's blonde hair was pulled back from his face in a short ponytail, and his body was skinniest of the three of us. I laughed sarcastically while Dex snatched the ten dollar bill from his hand.

"You guys are true pals," I replied. "Thanks for having my back."

"Don't cry about it," Dex said casually. "I would have helped if you bombed it."

"Look how much we got that tiny crowd going," Nate remarked excitedly. "Imagine what'll happen at the Screaming Rumble."

"No kidding!" Dex added. "Adam, you need to sing Lucid at the Rumble, too."

I quickly shook my head.

"No way—that's too much pressure."

"Come on, man. Don't wimp out."

Behind Dex, I saw someone walk around the corner of the building, but I recognized her in seconds.

"Can I get your autograph?"

Luna skipped toward me with a big smile, and I pulled her against me with my arm around her shoulders.

"You can have a lot more than that."

She kissed me while standing on her toes, and Nate groaned.

"Come on—time to chill in the van," he said.

Me, Dex, and Luna followed him across the parking lot to our old cargo van, which was black with REBEL RIOT spray-painted in bright green letters on each side. Me and the guys had bought it last summer to haul our band gear, but after graduation, it would also be our hazardous ride to California.

When Nate rolled back the side door, Luna climbed in first, followed by me, Dex and then Nate. The back of the van had seven large bean bags in the middle, and next to them was a blue cooler full of beer that Nate's older brother had bought us. For the next hour, we sat in the bean bags drinking and talking, until Dex finally grew restless.

"We should get out of here," he said anxiously. "We look like losers still hanging around."

"What's next, then?" Nate asked. "It's too early to go home."

"I don't know. Want to dumpster dive at Music World?"

I cheered loudly, and the four of us toasted our cans before we left.

PENS | Anna

Thursday morning, I climbed out of my car in the senior parking lot and jogged toward the yellow school bus to Bedford that sat in front of Gainesville High. After forgetting to set my alarm the night before, I was twenty minutes late, and felt relieved the bus hadn't left for the Hemingway exhibit without me.

"I'm sorry," I said breathlessly, stopping at the bus doors next to Mr. Emery. "I was up late, and—"

"Don't worry, Anna. You made it!"

My teacher was a tall, skinny man with blonde hair and a soft voice, and I could see in his smile that I hadn't upset him. I climbed the stairs into the bus, noticing several empty seats in the back, as well as Adam—who sat alone in the farthest seat on the left side, staring out the window wearing earbuds.

Don't be afraid... just be a light, remember?

I walked slowly down the aisle and slid into the empty seat across from him, hoping he'd ignore me. But his head immediately turned in my direction, and I forced a smile.

"You're late."

I blinked, surprised by his direct accusation.

"What?"

"I got here on time before you. Is the sky falling?"

I rolled my eyes. "No, I just forgot to set my alarm. It won't happen again."

"Oh. Were you studying?"

"No."

"Singing hymns?"

"What? No."

His flat expression was hard to read, and I wondered why he even cared that I was late.

"I bet you were selling drugs."

My jaw dropped as a wicked smile turned his mouth.

"If *I* was selling drugs, *you* were at Holmster's with the preppy boys," I countered.

Adam raised a brow, his nose wrinkling.

"Like *that* would ever happen."

"And then you went to the salon," I continued, "and got your hair gelled and spent the rest of the night like a pretty boy."

Adam turned from me in disgust, and I laughed quietly at my victory.

Think you can pester me so easily? Think again, Adam.

I reached in my backpack and grabbed my earbuds, then stared out the window for a while as I listened to music and watched Gainesville roll by. Eventually, I decided to look at Adam again, and I saw his head tilted back against the seat, his face mostly covered by the hood of his jacket. The black wires of his earbuds trailed down into his pocket, and to me, it looked like he could be sleeping.

Perfect! Now I can sketch.

After taking my drawing pencil and sketchbook from my bag, I flipped through the pages to my latest sketch, which was a ball gown with a beaded bodice, corset back, and flowing skirt. I spent the next few minutes working out the finer details until the empty spot beside me suddenly disappeared.

Looking right, I jumped, seeing Adam less than a few inches from me.

"You're into drawing?" he asked curiously.

His gaze dropped to my sketch pad, which I quickly closed.

"Yes, but it's nothing you'd be interested in."

I looked away and tried to decide how it felt having him so close, but he snatched the sketchbook from my hands.

"Adam!"

He ignored me as he flipped through the pages, causing my heart to pound.

"These are good," he said coolly. "Are you going to fashion school?"

I blinked, then laughed.

"Seriously? No—I'm going to study accounting."

"Oh, that's dull."

I frowned and took the sketchbook from his hands.

"I can make a great living as an accountant," I told him. "Designing dresses professionally is not very realistic."

Adam raised a brow, and I liked how the sunlight brightened his pale green eyes.

"Oh yeah? Says who? I'm sure a lot of people would think it's crazy I'm going to California with my band, but we're not afraid to give our music everything we've got."

The intensity of his stare somehow made my doubt feel ridiculous, and I looked down at my knees.

"What if you don't make it?" I asked. "Aren't you afraid to fail?"

Adam shrugged.

"It'll suck if things don't work out, but at least we tried."

I furrowed my brow as he went back to his seat, and for the rest of the ride, I tried not to think about my sketchbooks collecting dust one day. When the bus finally stopped outside the museum in Bedford, Mr. Emery gathered all of us on the sidewalk near an older woman in a blue suit who held a clipboard. Her salt and pepper hair was pulled back into a bun, and while she smiled at us, Mr. Emery gestured to her.

"Class, this is Elaina, our personal guide for the exhibit today," he announced.

"It's wonderful to meet you," she said afterward. "All the items you'll see today belonged to Hemingway and are on loan from his former estate in Key West. Follow me, please."

We walked a short distance from the sidewalk to the museum entrance, and inside the lobby, I admired the shiny marble floor and tall gray walls, which were lined with paintings and glass showcases. Elaina continued into a hallway ahead of us, and I stole a glance at Adam, who walked near me at the back of the group. He still had an earbud plugged in while tapping at his cell screen, and I wondered if he was just scrolling through music, or texting Luna.

It doesn't matter one bit what he's doing—I don't care.

I looked ahead stiffly, and a few minutes later, our group reached the Hemingway exhibit at the back of the museum. It shared a large room with a few other special exhibits, and in the far right corner, we spread out to see the recreation of Hemingway's office situated behind velvet ropes. His old black typewriter sat on top of a round wooden table with a tan woven rug beneath it, and three medium-sized white bookcases lined the walls under a stuffed antelope head.

"Everything you see was owned by Hemingway during his time in Key West," Elaina explained. "That Underwood typewriter, for example, he used to write 'To Have and Have Not' and a few other works. He even finished 'A Farewell to Arms' at the estate."

While she described in length the history of each item, I jotted down notes for the "surprise" report I expected Mr. Emery to assign. Elaina then led us in a Q&A session, and afterward, we were dismissed to explore and have lunch in the courtyard.

The sunny outdoor space was visible through the glass walls near the special exhibit room, and the courtyard had four beautiful trees surrounded by iron benches and silver tables in the center. When I stepped outside, I walked toward a shaded table and sat down, pulling my lunch sack from my backpack. I casually watched everyone else while I ate my sandwich and yogurt, though I suddenly realized that Adam was missing.

Is he walking around the museum?

I wondered about his absence for several minutes until I remembered not to care, and when I finished eating, I explored the museum for a few hours until it was time to leave. Although I hadn't been looking for Adam while I browsed, I still thought it was strange that I hadn't seen him anywhere, and after everyone boarded the bus, I finally started to worry. But minutes later, a wave of relief hit me when I saw Adam and Mr. Emery walk out of the museum doors. I watched them intensely until they reached the bus, and I stared out my window while Adam walked down the aisle. The stench of cigarette smoke immediately filled my nose, and despite not wanting to look at him, I did so with a disgusted expression.

"Got a problem?" he asked quickly.

"How many have you smoked?"

Adam grinned and said nothing.

"Where have you been this whole time?"

"Chilling by myself in a courtyard," he replied. "But Emery's ticked I took off to smoke—even though I'm legal."

"You're eighteen?"

"Yeah."

"Oh... me too."

Adam dug into his pocket suddenly, pulling out a red pack of cigarettes.

"Want one?" he asked.

I rolled my eyes and frowned.

"Definitely."

We turned away from each other, and for the next while, I listened to music and avoided sketching. The smell of the cigarette smoke gradually faded, and while

I enjoyed my newfound peace, a finger poked my arm and ended the illusion.

"Why do you believe in God and all that stuff?"

I blinked, almost certain I had imagined Adam's words.

"It's how I grew up," I replied. "But God is real."

He stared at me for a few long seconds, which caused my cheeks to flush.

"How do you know?"

"A lot of ways, I guess," I continued. "Someone got baptized last weekend after turning their life around from drugs, and they said their relationship with God saved them."

Adam furrowed his brow thoughtfully, and for the first time, I wished I could read his mind.

"Guess you'll have to see," he said.

I shrugged.

"Things like that happen all the time to Christians and in church, but I also have a prayer journal, and I've seen God answer *my* prayers."

"Seriously?"

"Yeah. One time my pastor challenged us to pray for something but not tell anyone about it. This was around my birthday last year, so I prayed for some really nice gel pens I saw at the store. I wanted to tell my mom because she kept asking me what I wanted, but I never told her about the pens. I didn't really think I'd get them, but when my birthday came... I did."

Adam's eyes widened. "What? You're lying!"

"No, I'm not! I was totally surprised, and when I asked her why she'd bought them, she said she had a strange feeling when she saw them."

"Are you sure you never told her?" he asked, amazed.

"Positive!"

Adam turned away from me and looked out the window, his expression confused and thoughtful. We didn't speak again for the rest of the drive, and when the bus finally arrived back at Gainesville High, school was already over. Once everyone had climbed off the bus, Adam and I exited last, and I kept pace with him as we walked across the parking lot.

"Why did you ask about my beliefs?" I asked.

"I don't know a lot of Christians, so I was just curious."

"Okay, but... what do *you* think about God?"

He shrugged as he gazed ahead distantly.

"There probably is something, but I don't really care."

"Are you sure? I can pray for you."

Adam stopped walking all of a sudden and I jumped back a few steps, finding the look in his eye slightly annoyed. I smiled awkwardly as I looked at him, trying to ignore how much I liked the gentle curve of his thick eyebrows, along with the fullness of his lips. But I sighed heavily when the orange butt of a cigarette slid between them.

"Pray I don't get lung cancer."

He looked bored before he walked away, and I turned in a different direction, frustrated until an idea struck.

He doesn't want lung cancer? Fine—there's only one way to prevent that. And I won't say a word about my prayers for him, because if they come true, he'll be so shocked—just like the gel pen story.

RISK | Adam

I slumped back into the old couch in my basement, staring at the ceiling while conversations I'd had with Anna yesterday repeated inside my head. I kind of hated them, because I wasn't exactly sure what to think about her anymore.

Being friendly doesn't make us friends. But maybe we can exist without suffocating each other now...

The sliding glass door opened across the room, and I looked to see Luna walking toward me. She sat down on the couch and hugged my right arm, but I didn't budge.

"You okay?" she asked.

"Yeah. Just thinking too much."

"About what?"

"Really dumb stuff."

"Oh—how'd the field trip go?"

I shrugged. "Wasn't bad, but Emery busted me for smoking."

Luna rolled her eyes. "Of course, he's such a control freak."

"Do you still have to go to the wedding?"

"Yep. It doesn't matter how much I beg my parents, they won't let me stay for the Rumble next weekend. I *have to go* to Ohio with them."

I groaned while Luna sat up and pulled a crumpled cigarette carton from the front pocket of her hoodie.

"They're so terrible," she continued. "I don't care about a cousin I met once years ago."

Luna pushed the cig between her lips as I grabbed a lime green lighter from the coffee table. She burned the tip quickly and took the first drag, then passed it to me.

"Do I smoke too much?" I asked.

She raised a brow. "No, why?"

I breathed in heavily, letting the toxins loosen up my mind and body.

"Just one of the dumb things I was thinking about."

We were quiet for a few long seconds, but it seemed Luna was busy thinking about something.

"Was Anna on the field trip?" she asked.

"Naturally—she'd never miss it."

"How annoying was she?"

"She wasn't, actually."

"Did you talk to her?"

"Yeah. She likes to draw. I didn't know that."

Luna's brow furrowed while she took another drag, then knocked off the ash in the ashtray on the coffee table.

"Draw what? Daisies?"

She laughed at her joke, and I frowned.

"No, dresses."

"Really? Like she's five?"

"The Hemingway stuff was cool," I said quickly. "They set up his office with the actual furniture he owned."

We talked about the exhibit for a few minutes, and smoked the cig until only the butt was left. After I snuffed it out, I couldn't ignore something that scratched at the back of my mind.

"Do you think it's crazy to be religious?" I asked.

Luna blinked, her eyes widening.

"Basically. Who wants a ton of freaking rules?"

"Do you know any religious people?"

"Just my aunt, but I don't see her that much."

"What's she like?"

"She's alright, but weird, too," Luna replied. "Why do you care about religion?"

"I don't really. It's just interesting to think about sometimes."

"Don't mention that to Anna," she said dryly. "She'll say you're going *straight* to hell."

I furrowed my brow, insulted and frustrated by Luna's know-it-all attitude towards her.

"She wouldn't say that. I know we're used to hating her, but she's not that bad anymore, okay?"

Luna's gaze shifted from mine, and she nodded quickly as she stood up.

"My parents want me home for dinner—I'll call you later."

Her tone was hardly convincing, and I watched as she walked across the room, slamming the glass door behind her.

●　●　●　●　●　●

I noticed more things about Anna now that I knew how much Luna truly hated her. During class Tuesday morning, I wondered if the small diamond studs in her ears were real, and I thought about her lips, which looked unusually glossy. These things distracted me from working on the presentation, and after a while, I felt a tap on my shoulder. Turning around, I looked into Anna's curious face.

"Want to go to the library?" she asked.

I nodded. "Yeah, sure."

We packed our things and got permission from Emery, then stepped into the hall. The library wasn't far from class, and while we walked, my mind blanked as I tried to think of something to say. But Anna seemed relaxed in the silence, and less than thirty seconds later, we crossed into the library. I followed her to the empty tables in the back, which each had four student laptops. I sat down across from her and opened a computer, leaning my backpack against the leg of the chair. When I glanced up, I saw Anna watching me.

"I get bored sitting in class all the time," she said tiredly.

"Oh... me too."

We started working quietly, and I stole looks at her face and lips, until I finally thought of something to say.

"Why did you want gel pens?"

"For my drawings."

"You color them?"

"The good ones," she replied. "But I've almost used them all up."

I looked back down at my laptop, but—

"You're in a band, right?"

"Yeah."

"What's it called?"

"Rebel Riot."

Her eyes filled with surprising intrigue, and for the first time, I wanted to read her thoughts.

"Do you write songs?" she asked.

"Just one so far."

"What's it about?"

I reached into my backpack and pulled out a black notebook, flipping to a certain page before sliding it toward her. My anxiety spiked while she read the lyrics, but when she finished, she smiled.

"This is great," she said happily. "I'm guessing it's about seeing something differently than another person?"

"Yeah, mainly. But it could mean a lot of things."

"What's it called?"

"Lucid."

Anna blinked, then raised a brow.

"*Lucid*? That's kind of fancy."

"Kinda trippy, too."

Anna slid the notebook back and leaned sideways, taking her sketchbook from her bag and opening it where a yellow sticky note stuck out.

"This is what I'm planning for my art showcase," she said excitedly.

She slid the sketchbook across the table, and I saw a drawing of three torso mannequins mounted on a rectangular platform. The left one wore a pink dress with long pink feathers all over it, and the middle dress looked like nothing but giant blue ruffles. The last dress was split in half and tie-dyed, with a lot of rhinestones on the top and bottom piece. Her designs surprised me since I knew Anna liked normal, trendy clothes, but these seemed straight out of a fantasy world—like *Alice in Wonderland.*

"It's called *haute couture*," Anna said, before I could speak.

I raised a brow. *"Haute couture?"*

"There's a long history to it, but these days, it's a special type of fashion for eccentric, one-of-a-kind pieces. I've always thought it was fascinating."

"How big are these going to be?"

"The mannequins? Just a few feet tall. We can make anything we want for our showcase, but it has to be three-dimensional and use repurposed materials. I'm going to carve the mannequins from Styrofoam, and then make the dresses from painted newspaper instead of fabric."

"Wow—I'm surprised you're not making a giant calculator."

Anna blinked, then rolled her eyes. We went back to working on the assignment until it was time to leave a half hour later, and when we stepped into the hall, I felt a crazy urge to tell her about the Screaming Rumble. But despite trying to ignore it, the words in my head fell out of my mouth.

"I'm singing Lucid at a club this weekend."

Anna suddenly looked at me, the same intrigue from earlier in her eyes.

"Really? Which one?"

"Loose Ella. It's thirty minutes from here, but my band is in a competition Friday night called the Screaming Rumble. It's a big deal and any prize money we win will help us make a demo in California."

"How? Do you want to record in a studio?"

"Yeah, but it's expensive. Demos don't have to be perfect, but we want to sound our best to get signed fast."

"Are you nervous to sing?"

"Mostly, but I'll get over it. I already sang Lucid for the first time last week, and I've decided to do it at the Rumble, too."

Anna's smile widened before she shook her head.

"I can't imagine ever singing in front of a crowd," she said anxiously. "How are you going to live when you get to California?"

"We're working on getting an apartment there right now, and Dex's uncle lives there and runs a landscaping company. We're going to work for him while trying to sign with a label."

"Dex is one of your band mates?"

"Yeah. He sings and plays the guitar like me, and then Nate is our drummer."

We reached the door to class a few seconds later, and when I grabbed the handle, I saw Anna turn away and face me.

"I've never been to a club," she said quietly.

"Really?" I replied with a grin. "You seem like the type who loves to go and twerk."

"What?" she countered, her jaw dropping.

"I'm kidding! Duh. But you should try it out."

"Twerking?"

"No—clubbing."

Excitement flooded through me even though I expected Anna to instantly refuse, but her face was thoughtful while she stayed silent.

"The competition does sound cool," she admitted at length. "But I don't know anything about clubbing and I'm sure my parents would say no."

"So what? You're eighteen."

"Yes, but—"

"You don't need their permission. You need to try it and see what it's like."

"Okay, but what if I don't want to dance, or drink, or—"

"You don't have to do any of that. You can just watch our set and then go home."

Anna bit her lip as she mulled over that tempting plan, and while I waited for an answer, I was surprised by how much I truly wanted her there Friday night.

"Luna will be there, right?" she asked hopefully.

"No. She's going out of town to a wedding."

"Okay—I'll go if I can bring a friend."

"Sure thing," I replied with a grin. "You'll survive, I promise."

BRAVE | Anna

After school that day, I ordered two white mochas at a small coffee shop, then sat at a table by the window while my thoughts whirled. Natalie would arrive at any minute, and I wondered how crazy I'd sound when I asked her to go to Loose Ella with me. Aside from my own personal interest, Adam had made a good point that gave me confidence: we didn't actually have to go clubbing—we could just watch his show and leave.

It's harmless enough to say yes to, right? I doubt we'll even be there that long...

When Natalie pulled into the parking lot a minute later, I tried to stay calm while she entered the cafe and sat down across from me. I smiled anxiously as she greeted me and took a sip from her white mocha, which I slid across the table a few seconds earlier.

"So, what's this thing you wanted to talk about?" she asked.

My heart pounded as my gaze dropped to the foam on top of my latte.

"Well..." I started. "You probably won't believe this, but Adam invited me to a club Friday night."

Natalie raised her eyebrows at once, her expression full of disbelief.

"No way! Seriously?"

"Yes! His band is in a contest called the Screaming Rumble, and... I actually *want* to go."

"Wow. Are you feeling okay?"

"Hear me out," I said quickly. "Of course I'm nervous about it, but Adam said we can just watch the show without drinking or dancing, and I think that's the perfect way to check it out, right?"

"*We?*"

Natalie's face grew more surprised, and I nodded slowly.

"That's another thing—I don't want to do this without you," I confessed. "Don't you think it'll be fun and a lot more safe if we go together?"

My best friend's mouth fell open a little, her speechlessness creating a few long, agonizing seconds for me.

"I can't go to a club," she insisted. "It's too risky, and my parents would say no."

"But we're eighteen and don't need their permission."

"I thought you didn't like Adam—or rock music."

"Adam isn't the worst anymore," I replied honestly. "We've gotten on better terms, and I don't care about the music—I just think it would be fun."

A thoughtful look came into Natalie's eyes as she took a few more sips from her white mocha.

"How far away is it?" she asked.

"Thirty minutes."

A few more tense seconds passed, then—

"Okay—I'll go."

"Great! What about your parents?"

"I don't know. But if I tell them we're going together and won't be there all night... I think they can handle it."

"Perfect! Mine should be fine, too," I said with a grin. "And we can still tell people we went 'clubbing' if we want."

Natalie laughed. "Yeah, I'm sure everyone at church will be impressed. What are we going to wear?"

"We'll need to look punk like Adam. Want to go thrifting before we leave Friday?"

"Of course! And then we can stop at the beauty store and get some spray-on hair dye."

"That's genius!" I replied with a gasp. "What's Jake going to think about this?"

"He'll probably want us to have police escorts," Natalie said, joking. "What do you think about going to prom with his friend, Sean?"

I frowned, the thrill of the moment suddenly dead.

"If I change my mind, I'll let you know."

"But maybe he's the answer to your prayers?" she suggested.

I shook my head. "I doubt it."

"Then who? There's only four weeks left until the dance."

"I don't know. But we'll see—okay?"

Natalie sighed with a nod, and I tried not to worry more about it than I already did.

* * * * * *

While I worked on my dress later that night, it felt incredible—and almost *impossible*—that in one afternoon, I had decided to go to a club Adam invited me to, and that by some miracle, my best friend had also agreed to go with me. But as fast and easy as it had worked out, I still hadn't mentioned my plans to my parents, despite coming home a few hours ago. Instead of telling them right away, I wasn't sure what my decision to go meant—if anything at all.

Does going to the club make me a bad Christian, even if I don't go wild?

I bit my lip while I hand-stitched the top of my dress skirt into the bottom of the bodice, believing I had made a terrible mistake.

What have I done? Everything about a club is wrong for us! We can't go to Adam's show—that's crazy!

I stuck my needle in the mannequin and walked toward my purse on the floor, taking out my cell phone to text Natalie. But just as I began to type a message, I glanced over at my Bible on my nightstand, suddenly struck by conviction.

If I don't go, how will I be a light? If I can't accept what he loves... how will Adam believe in God?

I slid my phone in my pocket and took a deep breath while my thoughts cleared. I suddenly realized that saying yes to the club meant a lot more than I thought it did—it created the best chance for Adam to open up to me, and possibly become saved. Without another thought, I left my room and walked downstairs to the living room, where I found my parents in their usual nightly routine. My dad laid back in his recliner while reading a book, and my mother sat on the end of the couch nearest to him, watching one of her favorite sitcoms. I stood in the arched entryway and watched them for a few seconds, then cleared my throat.

"Mom, dad—remember Adam, my project partner?"

Both of them looked at me, and my mother nodded.

"Yes, why?" she asked. "Did something happen?"

"Nothing bad. We've actually been getting along, and I want to go with Natalie Friday night to see his band play at a club."

The shock I expected to see spread across their faces, but before they could speak, I started to explain.

"He doesn't think God is real, so I need to go be a light," I urged. "You know I won't drink or do anything dangerous."

"What club is it?" my mom asked skeptically.

"It's called Loose Ella, and it's a half hour from here."

She turned to my dad, who stared at me thoughtfully.

"I'm surprised you want to go," he said calmly. "But I'm glad Natalie is going with you. You're an adult now and that's a smart decision."

I raised my eyebrows and nodded.

"So, you're both okay with it?"

"Not quite," my mom replied quickly. "When does it start, and how long will you be there?"

"I'm not sure when his band plays yet, but we're only going to stay long enough to see them, then we'll come home."

"What kind of band is it?"

"Rock."

My mom sighed heavily and looked at my dad again.

"You really don't care, Dave?" she said.

"I do care, but I think she's taken the right precaution. I know you'll be responsible, Anna."

"I will," I said gladly. "I just want to do this for Adam and see what it's like."

I turned away from them and went back to my room, where I celebrated my success with a small victory dance. When I started working on my dress again, I prayed my secret prayer for Adam—the one that would help him not get lung cancer.

HONEST | Adam

"Don't do it man," I threatened Nate. "Let me shoot you in the face for once."

My thumbs pounded the controller buttons while me, Nate, Dex and Luna sat in Nate's basement playing one of our favorite video games Thursday night. And what started as a fun time blasting aliens quickly turned into a bloodbath against each other.

"Blow up Nate with a grenade!" Luna shouted, elbowing me in the ribs. "Don't forget you have two left!"

She watched next to me on the couch while sipping a coke, her purple hair hanging loose around her face. Dex sat on the other side of her, and Luna liked helping us kill each other faster.

"Yeah, right!" Nate snapped. "I'll blast Adam right after I get Dex!"

He aimed his gun on the TV screen and ran toward the crumbling brick wall Dex hid behind, their avatars opening fire. I ducked behind a burned out car and tossed a grenade toward Nate, my blood racing in matter of seconds before it struck—blowing Nate into pieces. Dex laughed and jumped up, throwing his game controller on the floor.

"Take that loser!" he shouted. "You're not the best when you're a bunch of *bloody little pieces!"*

Nate glared while I stood up to high five Dex.

"I still have the most kills, so technically, I win," Nate said defensively.

Dex rolled his eyes, snorting.

"Whatever. Who wants pizza?"

The four of us walked upstairs, and in the kitchen, Luna turned the oven on to 450 degrees while Nate dug through the freezer for the pizza box.

"You got extra pepperonis?" Dex asked, opening the fridge.

"Yeah, in the back somewhere," Nate said, pulling out the pizza. "Grab the olives, too."

He put the box on the counter and slid the pizza onto a round baking sheet. Luna then dashed it with several spices she'd taken from the cupboard, and Dex layered on extra pepperonis and olives. After setting the timer, Nate put the pizza in the oven, and we all walked through the dining room and out the sliding glass door to the back deck. A bright light mounted to the side of the house lit up the deck and backyard, and Nate and Dex sat in green plastic chairs while me and Luna leaned against the railing. Immediately I felt the need to smoke, but as my fingers wrapped around the new pack of cigs in my pocket, I remembered how strange I had felt buying them yesterday—like I was doing something I shouldn't be.

The feeling doesn't mean anything... stop overthinking.

I bit the inside of my lip, wishing I could shut my brain off and relax.

"Did you buy prom tickets yet?"

I blinked, looking at Luna with a nod.

"Yeah—you told me to get them last week."

She shrugged. "Just checking."

I pulled the pack of cigs out of my pocket and pushed one between my lips, still unable to shake feeling off about it. But my anxiety only got worse when I realized I didn't have a lighter on me, either.

"Who are you guys taking to prom?" Luna asked Nate and Dex.

"Prom is *lame*," Dex said dramatically. "But maybe Lainey or Shayna. They're both bugging me about it."

Nate sighed and put his hands behind his head, annoyed.

"Can't we just have band practice that night?" he suggested.

Luna rolled her eyes, and I tried to look calm as I faced my best friends.

"Anyone have a lighter?" I asked, forcing myself to sound normal.

"No, man," Nate answered. "Probably one in the house, though."

I sighed and pulled the cig from my lips, stuffing it angrily back inside the carton.

"I still haven't heard from Steve," Nate said, worried. "He probably is a scam artist."

"He's not a scammer," Dex replied impatiently. "He told us that he has to get the money for the apartment before we can sign a lease. When he gets it, then we'll get the paperwork. It's only been four days since you mailed the money, right? It's almost to California, but not yet."

"Okay, but if he *does* steal our money, then we'll have to live out of the van until we find another place. And that'll suck big time."

Dex laughed, surprising the three of us.

"It would be totally rock and roll!" he shouted. "When we're rich and famous, we can tell everyone how we lived out of that rust bucket because we were so devoted to our music."

"We'll be lucky if it can even get us to California," Nate remarked.

While they argued, I kept wrestling with anxious thoughts until Luna pinched me on the arm.

"I'm ready to go home," she said.

"Sure—okay."

I followed her off the deck and around the side of the garage, where I noticed the tired and depressed look on her face.

"Don't let them get to you," I said casually. "Prom is what you make it, and we're going to have a lot of fun."

Luna sighed heavily.

"It's not just them," she replied. "I hate thinking about you leaving Gainesville soon."

"Yeah, but at least you can visit Cali when you're eighteen."

We reached the end of the driveway where her car was parked along the curb, and Luna leaned against the driver's door, glancing each way down the dark street lit by tall, dim metal lamps.

"That's another dumb thing," she said. "I shouldn't have to wait until my birthday in October to move out of state. My parents should just let me leave with you right after graduation."

She crossed her arms and I nodded, unable to admit that the guys didn't want her to tag along.

"It's probably a good thing since we're trying to figure out a lot right now," I replied uneasily. "But our apartment isn't that big, and if Steve is a scammer, then we *will* be living in the van."

I smiled a little and Luna rolled her eyes, her lips quickly meeting mine before she unlocked her car door.

"Don't put Lucid on the demo," she said suddenly. "I think the record execs will know it's your first song."

I blinked and raised my eyebrows.

"What? You said you loved it."

"It's okay, but if you want your best shot getting signed, I wouldn't put it on there."

"Why? I worked on it for a while, and a lot of people like it."

"I don't think it makes a lot of sense. Are you working on anything else?"

"Yeah... nothing solid yet."

My gaze dropped to the black pavement while I frowned, my hands becoming fists in my pockets as I struggled to let go of my disappointment.

"Don't be upset, Adam. I'm just trying to help. Do whatever you want."

I nodded and shrugged.

"No worries. Talk to you later."

Luna gazed at me, then sighed quietly before she sat in her car and closed the door. I waited on the street until she pulled away, watching her tail lights disappear once she turned onto another block. My fists loosened a little when I headed back across the driveway, still surprised that she hadn't loved my song as much as I thought.

The lyrics don't make sense? I mean, they're not totally obvious, but the meaning is still clear... right?

When I reached the deck, Nate and Dex were gone, and I suddenly remembered the pizza. I forgot about my disappointment for a second as I went into the house through the sliding glass door and found them eating in the kitchen.

"There's plenty left," Dex said, holding half-eaten crust. "But it's ice cold now."

I gave him a dirty look and walked to the pizza pan, grabbing a slightly warm piece.

"Luna left?" Nate asked.

I took a bite, nodding.

"You guys killed the mood about prom, and she's bummed I'm leaving soon."

"Did you tell her she can't live with us?" Nate said. "I mean, she's totally cool, but the apartment can't fit four people."

"I told her it was small, but I think we'll break up this summer, anyway."

"What?" Dex replied, shocked. "I thought you liked her night moves."

Nate laughed mockingly and pushed Dex's shoulder, causing him to stumble back a step.

"Stop listening to your dad's music," he said blandly. "It's aging you."

"I don't have a choice when he plays it all the time," Dex replied, shoving him back.

I finished my pizza slice, silently trying to pinpoint exactly where my feelings for Luna had spiraled—but there didn't seem to be a specific event, just a gradual disinterest.

"Sex isn't the issue," I said at length. "But I just found out she lied about liking Lucid. She told me she didn't understand it before she left, and that it shouldn't be on our demo."

"You serious?" Dex replied. "Lucid is such a crowd-pleaser. It's definitely going on the demo."

"Maybe it shouldn't," I argued. "Whose to say I didn't get lucky at Joe's Corner?"

"Luna isn't a musician," Nate said defensively. "Who cares what she thinks? We'll know for sure how people feel once you sing it at the Screaming Rumble."

I frowned, shrugging.

"Why don't you date Anna?"

Every muscle in my body tensed as Dex's random question felt like a bucket of cold water dumped on me.

"*What?*"

"Don't play dumb! You guys are friendly now and she's always been hot."

I shook my head, trying to look disgusted.

"Hell *no*—I'd never date her in a million years," I replied.

"Don't sweat it," Nate said with a smirk. "We know she'd turn you down, anyway."

My brow twitched angrily as the memory of asking Anna to the club—and the fact that she said *yes*—passed through my mind. Clearly, I wasn't so repulsive anymore.

"Anna will be at the Rumble this weekend," I blurted.

The smug expressions of my best friends vanished, and both stared at me in surprise for several long seconds.

"Anna Holbach is *not* coming to the Screaming Rumble," Nate stated in disbelief. "We can't wash the whole place in holy water."

"Well, she is," I snapped, ignoring his sarcasm. "Obviously she didn't turn me down when I asked."

"You've got a huge pair," Dex said, impressed. "But I'll believe it when I see it. I bet she'll chicken out, though, and then you won't have to admit you lied."

"I'm not lying. She *will* be there," I insisted. "She's even bringing a friend."

"Sure," Nate replied casually. "I'll believe it when I see it, too."

"Fine—count on it."

Tense silence filled the kitchen then, but Dex broke it when he suggested going back downstairs to play our video game. We enjoyed the next few hours without mentioning Anna, and when I left Nate's house around 2 a.m., a whole new anxiety stirred in me about the weekend. Even though I wanted Anna to go to Loose Ella for a lot of reasons, I wasn't sure how good I could hide that she wasn't my dreaded project partner anymore.

In fact, it was scary how my honest feelings had changed about her so quickly.

She understood Lucid.

CLUB | Anna

After school that Friday, Natalie and I went thrifting for punk clothes and bought temporary hair dye before driving to my house to wait until 9 p.m., when the Screaming Rumble began. We sat on my bed watching TV and eating snacks later that evening, and when I checked my phone, I nudged Natalie with my elbow.

"Ready to become Natzilla?" I said, trying to ignore the butterflies in my stomach.

"Totally, Anferatu," she replied with a laugh. "I still can't believe we're going to a club tonight."

"I know. But if it's super weird or creepy—we'll leave right away."

"Obviously."

I shut off the TV and we climbed off the bed, grabbing our thrift store clothes and facing away from each other to change. When we turned around a few minutes later, I stared at Natalie's large Def Leppard t-shirt and tight red jeans, the extra fabric of her shirt tied into a knot at her hip. She stared back at my black tank top and yellow sequined skirt, along with the fishnet stockings I wore that I used for Halloween last year.

"I think we're definitely going to blend in!" she exclaimed.

"Yeah! And once we do our hair and make up, no one will have a clue who we really are," I added with a grin.

We left my room with the bag of temporary hair dye and walked into the hallway bathroom, where I set the two spray cans on the sink counter. I then sat on the toilet lid, looking nervously at Natalie while I felt the butterflies in my stomach again.

"What color do you want?" she asked.

My gaze flashed from her to the blue and pink cans.

"Hmm—pink!"

Natalie grabbed the large sheet of tin foil I'd placed on the counter earlier and slipped it beneath a layer of my hair. I squeezed my eyes shut as she held the pink can and shook it, then worked her way around my head. I tried not to imagine the worst as she worked quickly—reminding myself that the dye was temporary, and no one actually cared what I looked like at the club. But when Natalie stepped back a minute later, I was afraid to move.

"Alright—take a look!"

I stared at her happy face before I jumped in front of the mirror, frantically studying the bright pink highlights in my dark hair until I grinned.

"Wow, these look so cool!"

"Awesome! It's pretty easy once you get the hang of it."

"Good, because now it's *your* turn."

Natalie looked at me bravely as she sat down on the toilet lid, and I grabbed the blue spray can and tin foil. I took a deep breath before I carefully sprayed the first blue streak into her blonde hair, then the next. Natalie sat quietly while I worked and didn't close her eyes, but like she said, creating the highlights quickly became easy. For less than two minutes, I moved around her head and sprayed until I was finally satisfied.

"It's a masterpiece!"

Natalie jumped in front of the mirror like I did, and I smiled as I watched her face glow.

"I *love* the blue!" she gushed. "Highlights were the best idea!"

"We should be Anferatu and Natzilla more often," I teased. "This is fun!"

I opened the cabinet under the sink and pulled out a large cosmetic bag full of Halloween and barely used makeup from the last few years, and after we experimented for a while, Natalie settled on silver glitter eye shadow and purple lip gloss, while I chose blood red eyeshadow and pink lipstick. We then left the bathroom and started down the staircase to the foyer.

"Did I tell you Adam is singing tonight?" I asked excitedly.

My best friend shook her head, and when we reached the bottom of the steps, I saw a strange smile on her face.

"What?"

"Do you think Adam is cute?" she asked casually.

I gasped dramatically as my mouth fell open.

"Are you serious? That's crazy!"

"Not even a little?"

"No way! Adam is *not* my type," I insisted. "Why would you think that?"

"Well, you've been getting along with him and now we're going to his show, so... I was just curious. Besides, Adam isn't that ugly."

My eyes widened while I tried to look horrified despite all the times I had admired almost every part of his face.

"Are you kidding me? He's not even Christian," I replied defensively.

"But if he was... would you date him?"

I laughed dismissively and rolled my eyes.

"That's crazy," I said. "Can we go and talk about something else?"

Natalie smiled innocently and shrugged.

"Sure, let's go!"

*   *   *   *   *   *

When we reached Loose Ella, the large parking lot with almost a hundred cars was nearly full. I found an empty space beneath a yellow streetlamp at the back of the lot, and Natalie twisted around in her seat, staring at the club through the back windshield.

"I hope they have good security," she said nervously.

I nodded. "Me too."

We climbed out of my car and walked closely together across the dark parking lot, our eyes fixed on the club, which sat longer than it was wide. A neon blue sign that read LOOSE ELLA hung above the front door, and the brick building was lit from the ground by multicolored lights, and had a few blacked out windows.

After we stepped onto the sidewalk in front of the door, Natalie reached into the small purse at her hip and took out her cell phone.

"Want to take pictures to document this?" she asked excitedly.

"Totally!"

We wrapped an arm around each other and smiled normally for a few photos before we stuck out our tongues and made silly faces. Afterward, we finally walked inside Loose Ella, and immediately entered a black room covered in band posters with bright purple fluorescent lights on the ceiling. A woman in a pink tube top with bleached blonde hair stood behind a boxy desk, and across the front of it, a long banner had SCREAMING RUMBLE written on it in graffiti-style letters. When we approached the desk, I tried to hide my anxiety as the hostess stared at us with an unfriendly expression.

"Hi," Natalie said carefully. "How much to watch the contest?"

The woman crossed her arms and raised a brow.

"You girls have ID?"

Natalie quickly dug our driver's licenses out of her purse and handed them to the hostess, who looked them over.

"Ten bucks a piece," she said.

Natalie then handed her a twenty dollar bill, and the woman pointed to the right side of the room with her thumb.

"The dance room is at the end of the hall. If anything happens, *don't* call the police. Ask the bartenders for Hans—he'll take care of any problems."

Natalie and I nodded before we turned away and entered the hall. When we were out of sight, I looked at my best friend in shock.

"I can't believe they don't want us to call the police!" I said in a loud whisper.

"I know," Natalie replied with a frown. "But aren't you curious about Hans? Sounds like he's a beast."

I sighed and gazed down the dark hall, which had a bright blue door with a diamond-shaped window at the end. Loud music vibrated through the walls, and as we drew closer to the dance room, my nose wrinkled from the strong odor of sweat and smoke. When Natalie pushed the door open, we stepped into the lounge area between the bar, stage, and dance floor. Flashing lights lit up the countless faces around us, and although I felt easily overwhelmed by everything I saw and smelled, a small part of me grew increasingly excited.

"Where's Adam?" Natalie asked loudly.

"I'm not sure. Maybe somewhere near the stage?"

We walked toward the left end of the room near the stage and dance floor, and after making our way around the dancing crowd, I saw three teenage boys beside the stage. Two of them faced me with their backs, and the third leaned against the wall with his arms crossed. Although they were impossible to identify from where I stood, a strong feeling in my gut told me to approach them.

"I think I see them over there—let's check it out!"

Natalie followed me as I walked closer to them, my eyes studying the black-haired boy who leaned against the wall in a striped gray t-shirt and dark jeans. When I was less than ten feet away, a bright yellow light glided over his face, and I grinned as I knew I'd found Adam.

"Hey!" I exclaimed. "It's me!"

Adam looked in my direction with no hint of recognition, and when his friends turned and stared at me, I forced myself to wait out the awkwardness for several long seconds.

"Adam, don't you recognize me?"

He blinked before his eyes widened and he pushed off the wall.

"Wait—how—*Anna?*"

I laughed as he walked toward me and Natalie, who stood at my side.

"Yes, it's me! And this is my best friend, Natalie."

Adam's gaze remained locked on my form while he stood a few inches away.

"I can't believe it," he said, stunned. "You came—you *look*—"

"I'm glad you're impressed," I replied with a grin.

He then looked down at my skirt and felt it between his fingers, causing my cheeks to burn as his hand brushed against my thigh.

"Where'd this come from?" he asked.

"Um—the thrift store."

He let go of my skirt and pinched a chunk of my hair.

"You dyed your hair, too?"

"It's temporary," I admitted. "Who are these guys? Your bandmates?"

Adam nodded and gestured to the blonde one on the left, then the spiky-haired one on the right.

"Yeah—that's Nate and Dex. They're my best friends."

I smiled awkwardly at them while they stared without a word.

"What do you think of this place?" Adam asked excitedly.

"There's a lot going on, but I think it's cool! When do you guys play?"

"We're fourth in the lineup," he replied. "And there's five other bands competing tonight."

"What are the prizes?" Natalie asked curiously.

"First place is a grand, second is five hundred, and third is two-fifty. You guys are going to dance when we're jamming on stage, right?"

I raised an eyebrow and looked at Natalie before laughing.

"We're here to *see* the show—remember?"

"Yeah, but the dance floor is a lot of fun..."

"No thank you. Just play the guitar, okay? We'll figure out what to do."

"Lame, but whatever. The contest is starting soon, so you should grab a couch and get cozy."

I stuck my tongue out at him and looped my arm around Natalie's, then walked with her to the lounge area on the other side of the dance floor. We quickly claimed a stiff, two-person couch with a few large stains and got the attention of a waitress, who took our order of coke and mozzarella sticks.

"I hope it's safe to eat here," Natalie said, her nose slightly wrinkled.

We talked loudly for ten minutes until the booming music suddenly faded, and the flashing lights focused on a man with green hair in black suit who stood center stage with a microphone.

"Do you know what time it is?" he announced. "If you're ready for *the Rumble*, let me hear you SCREAM!"

Almost a hundred voices pierced my eardrums before I could block them out with my fingers, but Natalie hardly seemed to notice.

"The first band tonight is Midnight Ransom. They're local and have played all around the state. They say their music is reminiscent of Black Sabbath, but I'll let *you* decide. Where are you, Midnight?"

The atmosphere grew tense while three gangly guys emerged from the darkness on the left side of the stage. They barely acknowledged the crowd as two of them stood in front of microphones with their guitars, and the third sat behind the drum set. To me, they looked like ghouls.

"Release your loudest howl for MIDNIGHT RANSOM!" the host shouted.

I managed to plug my ears before everyone screamed again, and during the middle of the band's first song, Natalie and I got our coke and mozzarella sticks—which we tried cautiously.

"It's delicious!" I exclaimed, savoring the warm, tasty cheese on my tongue.

Natalie nodded. "It's so good! Six of these might not be enough."

While we ate, we watched all the sweaty bodies that danced chaotically on the dance floor, and soon, Natalie turned to me.

"Think we should try it out there?" she asked bravely. "It looks like everyone is just jumping around."

My eyes widened as I anxiously considered her suggestion.

"Are you sure? There's no space between anyone!"

"We can dance in front of the stage when Adam plays and stay away from the crowd. Come on! What do you think?"

The booming music drowned out the whine that escaped my throat as my gaze shifted from Natalie to the crazed crowd. Although there was a large gap between them and the stage, the thought of being so close to either felt daunting.

"Um—well—okay!"

Natalie squealed and hugged me while my heart pounded, and for the next forty-five minutes, we waited until the green-haired host finally introduced Rebel Riot.

"That's Adam's band!" I shouted excitedly.

My best friend and I watched as Adam, Nate, and Dex walked onto the stage with rock n' roll hand salutes before they began setting up their instruments. Naturally, my gaze lingered on Adam as he stood beneath the lights, his expression calm despite many eyes on him while he tuned his electric guitar.

"The dudes of Rebel Riot are the youngest rockers we have tonight," the host said, teasing. "Nate, Dex and Adam are practically children, but don't be disappointed! They say their music is as wild and soulful as Guns and Roses, but that's some big talk if you ask me!"

The crowd roared eagerly, and afterward, Adam started their first song with a pulsing riff that sent a surge of energy through me.

"Ready to dance?" I asked, grabbing Natalie's wrist.

"Yeah! Let's go!"

We raced from the couch to the dance floor and made our way around the crowd to the front of the stage. When we stood in the gap, I stared up at Adam, who focused intensely on the neck of his guitar while he rapidly switched between chords. Natalie raised her arms and started swaying her hips, and after a few hesitant seconds, I joined her. My heart pounded while I danced in front of the crowd, but I closed my eyes and felt alone with the pulsing music that flowed in and around me. I felt my stress and fear evaporate as the minutes passed, and I escaped to a place of joy as I moved in effortless ways to the music. But when their first song ended, my bliss was suddenly cut short when Natalie grabbed my arm.

"What's wrong?" I asked, staring into her red face.

"I'm dying in here! Let's get some water!"

She pulled me behind her as we jogged around the dancing crowd and made it to the bar on the opposite side of the room. There, we slid onto two empty stools and ordered ice water, which she and I practically gulped down.

"I didn't notice how sweaty I was," I confessed in surprise. "Once I closed my eyes and started moving, I forgot everything else!"

"Me too—almost," she replied with a grin. "When will Adam sing?"

"I'm not sure, but he wrote the song. It's called Lucid."

"Really? What's it about?"

I stuck out my tongue and shook my head.

"When you hear it, you can tell me! It could mean a lot of things, honestly."

Natalie rolled her eyes, but horror filled her face when she glanced over my shoulder.

"I think some guy behind you is going to die," she said.

My blood raced as I slowly turned and saw a young man with his eyes closed and mouth open bent over a few feet away. He had one hand on his stomach while the other pressed against a bar stool, and I thought his expression seemed strangely bland.

"What's wrong with him?" I asked frantically.

"I don't—*gross!*"

Behind me, I heard something wet smack against the tiled floor, followed by a sour odor in the air.

"Let's get out of here!" Natalie exclaimed.

We slid off our stools and jogged back to the dance floor just as Rebel Riot's second song ended. When Natalie and I returned to the gap, I struggled not to think about the vomit that had splattered so close to me, but those thoughts disappeared as Adam spoke into the microphone.

"Lucid is our last song," he said coolly. "It's a personal piece I wrote a while ago, and it's not like anything you've heard tonight."

The chaos of the dance floor died down while Adam began to strum a slow, haunting intro on his guitar. Dex soon joined with a quiet riff that intensified, and after their instrumental opening, Adam finally started to sing. His youthful, husky voice filled the club effortlessly, and I felt unable to move as I stared at him, studying each emotion that flickered across his face as I soaked in every word. But the atmosphere of Loose Ella gradually faded as I slipped into some piece of the future, where I saw Adam on stage inside a large stadium, several years older and miserably famous while he played for tens of thousands.

They're going to be famous one day. Everything they hope for... the risk will pay off.

I returned to reality when Adam's voice disappeared, and the crowd shouted their approval behind me at the end of the song. Adam grinned while he saluted everyone with rock n' roll hand gestures, and the host reappeared from behind the curtain to share his praise also.

"I think they're going to win!" Natalie said. "Everyone loved Lucid!"

"I think so too! Adam sounded great!"

The boys left the stage when the next band was announced, and Natalie and I followed them until we caught up to their group. Adam, Nate, and Dex were too busy high-fiving each other to notice us at first, but when Adam saw me, he stepped toward us with a proud smile.

"What'd you think of that?" he asked excitedly. "Probably our best performance yet!"

"Absolutely!" I agreed blindly. "Everyone thought you were incredible!"

"We are," Dex added in a cocky tone. "But I think you're really Anna Holbach's evil twin."

I blinked and raised a brow.

"Oh, yeah? Maybe you're right."

Adam looked at me in surprise while Nate and Dex laughed.

"Let's get some cool air," Nate insisted. "It's like an oven in here."

Natalie and I followed them into a dark hallway that led to a white door with a glowing red EXIT sign above it, which was already propped open with a beer bottle. After walking outside, the five of us stood in a circle behind the building, and I took in a deep breath of much needed fresh air. The sounds of the city were muffled through the dense tree line near us, and the brightness of the moon provided most of our light.

"So... how was clubbing?" Adam asked curiously.

"I actually had a lot of fun," I replied happily. "The only bad part was when a guy puked next to me at the bar."

"That's totally normal here," Nate said indifferently.

"He probably drank too much," Natalie added, groaning. "It was disgusting—I saw the whole thing."

"Adam barfs a lot, too," Dex said with a laugh. "Remember Shayna's party?"

I looked at Adam with a raised brow, and he shrugged.

"Couldn't help it. Those jello-shots were loaded."

I rolled my eyes.

"So, how do we vote for you?" I asked.

Adam reached into his pocket and took out a folded green piece of paper.

"Text our band code to the number on there," he said eagerly.

After opening the flier, I held it out for Natalie, who texted our vote through her phone and mine.

"When will they announce the results?" she asked.

"The winners will be posted on the website in a few days," Adam replied, annoyed. "They have a stupid delay period because of a big fight last year."

"Really? How bad was it?"

"Someone had their teeth knocked out and a bottle smashed over their head," Dex said with enthusiasm. "Hans got it all under control, but someone still called the cops and a lot of people went to jail."

"Wow—I'm glad the place didn't get shut down," I replied.

"You're telling me. We need some prize money for Cali."

"I'm sure you're going to win first place," I said confidently. "Everybody loved your songs—especially Lucid."

Natalie gently nudged me with her elbow and showed me her cell screen, which read 11:49 p.m.

"We should probably get going," she said in a hushed tone. "I told my parents I would be home before midnight."

My eyes widened as I realized the time, and I nodded.

"Thanks for inviting me, but we need to leave," I told Adam quickly. "You sounded great tonight."

"What's your number?" he asked carefully. "You know—for project stuff."

I blinked, surprised that anything project related had crossed his mind right then.

"Give me your phone and I'll type it in."

While I saved my number inside his phone, the silence of the group was noticeable until Natalie and I said our goodbyes, then we walked around the corner of the building.

"I think our parents will be proud," I said with a smile. "Even though you'll be home late, we didn't get into any trouble."

"Nope," she replied happily. "I'd say it was a success. But isn't it strange Adam wanted your number?"

Without thinking, I shrugged and shook my head.

"No—he said it was for the project. How exciting."

I glanced at Natalie, who rolled her eyes with a knowing expression.

"Believe that if you want, but even if you don't like him, I definitely think he likes you."

NUMBER | Adam

The digital clock next to my bed read 10:54 a.m. when I woke up the next morning. My pillow was halfway over my head as I lay on my mattress without covers, which I'd kicked off during the night. When I opened my eyes, I instantly remembered the guys ribbing me about asking for Anna's number last night.

Pretty dumb excuse. Anna probably knew it had nothing to do with the project. What an idiot...

I squeezed my eyes shut, unable to sleep as my mind replayed that moment over and over. If Anna had been able to see through me... I couldn't help but wonder how she felt about it.

I bet she hasn't been able to stop laughing. I'm really pathetic.

After sulking in bed for a while, I dragged myself into the private bathroom connected to my room, where I stripped off my boxers and turned on the shower. I waited until steam started filling the room before I stepped in; the hot water helping me feel more alive as it struck my head and back. My long hair covered my face while I started washing up, and for a minute, I managed to relive the excitement of our performance all over again.

We'll definitely come in second place, though maybe... first... if we're lucky.

After fifteen minutes, I left the shower and wrapped a towel around my waist, then walked back into my room. It was still dark with the blinds closed, and my mattress laid on the floor surrounded by dirty clothes, magazines, and junk food wrappers. The white walls were mostly bare except for a few band posters, and a short table in the far right corner had a small flat screen and gaming system on it. I walked to my closet and pulled out a red shirt, then grabbed jeans from the floor and got dressed. I picked up my cell and cigs from next to my bed, stuffing them in my pocket as I left my room.

While I headed downstairs, the smell of fried hamburger filled the house, and I found my mom stabbing at ground beef on the stove with a spatula. Even though it was almost noon, she wore a blue bathrobe, and her brown and blonde streaked hair was lazily clipped back.

"When did you get home last night?" she asked me.

I opened the fridge and took out an energy drink.

"Around one, I think."

"How did the contest go?"

"It was amazing—probably our best show yet. Anna came."

My mom looked at me in surprise while I leaned back against the counter, popping the tab on my drink.

"What did she think?" she asked curiously. "Things must be getting a lot better between you two."

"They are, and she said she had fun. She got all dressed up too. She looked completely different."

"What are you doing tonight?"

"Not sure. I might do homework with Anna."

"Homework? On Saturday?"

I shrugged. "It's no big deal—I like the project we're working on. Nate and Dex are busy."

"Okay. I'm making spaghetti for lunch. It will be done soon."

I took a gulp of my energy drink and left the kitchen, turning the corner to the open staircase that led into the basement. I jogged toward the couch at the bottom of the steps and collapsed into it, pulling my cigs and cell phone out of my pocket.

Maybe I should text Anna about the project so it doesn't seem like I was lying.

When I opened a new text message, my pulse raced. No matter what I wrote or how casual it sounded, I felt convinced that my feelings toward her would be screamingly obvious. But after a few minutes, I managed to type three words.

ME: hey. it's adam.

The next five minutes were pure torture.

ANNA: Hi. What's up?

ME: not much. get home alright?

ANNA: Yes. You?

ME: yep. got home around 1 a.m. you busy tonight?

ANNA: No. Why?

ME: want to work on the project?

ANNA: You want to do hw on a Saturday?

I rolled my eyes, wishing my usual habits weren't so obvious to everyone.

ME: just thinking we could get ahead.

ANNA: Ok. That's probably a good idea. Where do you want to meet?

ME: ember cafe at 6?

ANNA: Sure. See you then.

I smiled a little as my anxiety mixed with pride, and I took a cig from the carton, then pushed it between my lips. After burning the tip orange, the nicotine hit my brain quickly, and I closed my eyes, my mind growing more relaxed. But less than a minute later—a strange wave of dread struck me.

What the...?

I tried to ignore it as I inhaled deeply for more nicotine, but a scratch at the back of my throat made me start coughing *hard*. My cig fell out of my mouth while I beat my chest with my fist, and after several minutes, I could finally breathe normally again. My body shook from surprise and exhaustion as I picked up my cig from the floor and threw it angrily across the room.

Screw this!

I sunk back into the couch and crossed my arms, glaring at the blank TV across from me. As much as it sucked to have my quick hit of bliss ruined, I couldn't explain why everything had gone wrong with it lately.

● ● ● ● ● ●

Shortly after 6 p.m., I chained my bike to a metal rail in the parking lot behind the Ember Café. The small coffee shop wasn't that busy, and I walked through the back door into the middle of the shop. An empty table sat in the corner away from the front window, and after sitting down, I slid off my backpack and took out my laptop. I waited a few minutes before the bell above the front door jingled, and Anna stepped inside. She waved at me as she walked to the front counter, and a few minutes later, she came to the table and sat down.

"I think I can finish the essay today," she said excitedly. "Presentations start next week, but I'm almost done."

"Exactly. That's why I thought we should do this."

Anna grinned, and while she took her school things out of her backpack, I noticed the faded pink highlights in her hair, which I liked.

"What did you order?"

"A white mocha," she replied. "I'm guessing you don't drink coffee or tea?"

"Nope. Iced tea isn't bad, though."

"I come here a lot with Natalie. We were here a few days ago when we decided to see your show."

"Do you still think the club was fun?" I asked curiously.

Anna nodded. "Definitely! And I didn't tell you last night, but... *we danced.*"

My eyes widened in surprise, my body feeling paralyzed while a barista delivered Anna's drink in a ceramic mug.

"You *what?* You *danced?*"

"We did! Right in front of the stage. I wasn't sure if you saw us, but we only danced to your songs."

"No—I didn't," I said. "You should have told Dex last night. He would've been so proud."

Anna smiled a little and tucked her hair behind her ear while staring into her latte.

"Are you proud?" she asked shyly.

"Yeah... of course."

Our eyes stayed on each other for a few long seconds until Anna quickly started typing on her laptop. I looked down at mine and tried to start working, but spent the next few minutes waiting for the awkwardness to pass. After a while, the tension I felt disappeared, and Anna peeked up from her computer screen.

"How far are you with the presentation?" she asked calmly.

"I'm almost done," I replied a second later. "But the way Emery wants it formatted is complicated."

She nodded and went back to working, her cheeks still pink like they had been for a while.

Anna's glad that we're here, so it wasn't stupid to ask for her number, thankfully. But it seems like she... no—don't kid yourself.

While I worked on formatting the presentation, it felt impossible not to obsess about her feelings toward me, though I eventually relaxed when I started looking at band equipment online. A half hour passed before Anna stopped typing like a machine, her expression pleased when she looked at me.

"The essay is finally done," she said happily. "Did you finish already?"

"Yeah," I replied with a nod. "Nice job."

"Thanks. Um—do you like ice cream?"

I blinked, my eyebrows furrowing.

"Of course, everyone does."

"Want to get some down the street, then?"

"Sure."

We packed our things in silence, and when we left the cafe, I was secretly grateful Anna had created an excuse to spend more time together. The street was full of other people as we walked down it, and while I failed to think of anything interesting to say, Anna wasn't fazed.

"Writing any new songs?" she asked curiously.

"Yeah—working on one right now, but it kind of sucks. Good thing a lot of crappy songs are used to fill albums, though."

She laughed. "Totally. Some of my CDs only have a few good songs on them. I guess it's impossible to write hits all the time."

"A good song doesn't have to be a hit," I replied with a slight grin. "A lot of mainstream music isn't that good."

"Maybe," Anna replied thoughtfully. "Though I guess someone could think your new song is amazing, even if you don't."

I shot her a doubtful look, but liked what she said anyway. We stopped in front of the old-fashioned bakery a few seconds later, and inside, Anna ordered two scoops of cookie dough, while I chose chocolate chunk in a waffle cone. When we exited, we turned the corner of the building and sat down on a wooden bench that faced the street.

"How's your art project coming?" I asked.

Anna sat a few inches away from me, and she ate a large scoop of ice cream before answering.

"It's going great. I just have one more dress to finish."

"Where's the showcase going to be?"

"In the conference room beside the library. We're putting our projects in there next week."

"Cool. I still can't believe how crazy *hot culture* is."

"You mean *haute couture?*" Anna said, laughing. "It's meant to be wild and unique, but it's still an art."

"Oh, kind of like my music."

"Exactly. Did I tell you I'm making my own prom dress?"

I raised a brow suddenly. "Seriously? You're making a real dress?"

"Yep—but I'm following a pattern, so it's not as complicated as it sounds. I'm still adding my own ideas, though."

I tried to imagine the kind of dress she would make as I ate a few more bites of ice cream, but the possibilites were too endless.

"What's it look like?"

"Are you going to prom?" she asked.

"Yeah."

"Then you'll see it when I'm wearing it."

I looked at her and frowned.

"Tell me."

"No."

"Do it."

"No."

Her nose wrinkled in annoyance, and I smirked.

"Who are you going to prom with?" I asked, keeping my voice flat.

"I'm not sure yet."

"Why? Did a ton of guys ask?"

My muscles tensed at the thought of her attention being taken by someone else that night, but Anna laughed and rolled her eyes at my semi-joke. Truthfully, I wouldn't be surprised if ten guys had already asked her—all of them probably a much better choice than me.

"I'm not sure because it may be better if I go alone."

Her voice was serious as she looked into her ice cream cup, and I fought an anxious urge to ask who wanted to go to prom with her.

"I got accepted to Strathsmith a few months ago," she said, changing the subject.

"Oh, that's a good school. No fashion, then?"

She shrugged. "I'll keep drawing, but accounting will be my career."

"Okay. Are you going to church tomorrow?"

"Of course—why?"

"Well... what would happen if you never went back?" I asked curiously.

Anna's eyebrows furrowed while different emotions flickered across her face.

"My parents and church family would be sad," she replied thoughtfully. "They'd probably pray for me to come back."

"What else would they do?"

"What do you mean? I'm not going to be kidnapped or whacked," she said with a laugh.

I smiled a little. "You sure?"

"Positive!"

We got up from the bench and walked around the corner of the building, where Anna chucked her plastic spoon and ice cream cup into a garbage can before we walked back toward the cafe.

"You should keep the pink highlights," I said casually. "They looked great last night, and I can still kind of see them."

Anna smiled as she twirled a piece of pinkish hair around her finger.

"I thought they were pretty cool," she admitted. "When did you start dying your hair?"

"Last year, but the roots look like crap right now."

"I like the black. It looks good on you."

I glanced at her curiously, wanting to know what she thought about the rest of me. When we reached the cafe, Anna stepped off the sidewalk and crossed a short distance to her car.

"See you Tuesday, Adam."

I waved my hand once as she smiled and slid into the driver's seat, her gaze flashing to me a few times before she drove off. And no matter how impossible it seemed, I started to believe that Anna Holbach shared the same secret feelings I had.

FREEZE | Anna

When I met Natalie in the lunch line on Monday, her face filled with surprise while she stared at the fresh pink highlights in my hair.

"You're keeping the pink?" she asked, her voice high-pitched.

"Why not?" I replied innocently. "There's still plenty of dye left in the can."

"*Sure.* Does this have anything to do with Adam?"

I shook my head, though I knew my odds of fooling her were next to zero.

"He did want my number for *homework* after all," I said, bored. "He texted me on Saturday and we worked on our project at the Ember Café."

"Seriously?"

"Yep."

We moved ahead a few steps in line, and I tried not to frown while Natalie's surprised expression turned into satisfaction.

"I'm still right," she replied confidently. "Adam does *like you*, and working on the project was just an excuse to *hang out* with you."

"That's not true," I countered. "He's taking the project seriously because he wants to graduate."

Natalie shrugged and grinned slyly.

"He probably has a few good reasons, Anna."

I rolled my eyes, my frown finally breaking through. Although it was easy to see how my best friend had put the pieces together, and I had somewhat suspected Adam's feelings—our time before graduation was running out, and admitting to his and my feelings felt dumb, like an unnecessary jump into an endless pit. We were silent while we reached the front of the line, and after filling our trays and paying, we walked across the cafeteria to an empty round table. I sighed heavily when we sat down, knowing I couldn't hide all my thoughts from Natalie any longer.

"No matter how Adam or I feel, there's a lot of complications," I confessed. "First, Adam isn't really the type of guy I should be with, and second, he's moving thousands of miles away after graduation. Not to mention the third problem, his girlfriend—*Luna.*"

The noise of the cafeteria disappeared while the air around us grew tense. I watched Natalie consider these challenges silently as I took the first few bites of my lunch.

"I get it, but you don't actually need to date," she replied at length. "I just thought it was amazing—and *funny*—how you both went from hating each other to having a crush."

"It is strange, but I've been trying not to think about it. Graduation is two weeks away, and I don't want to do anything with Adam outside of school anymore. We just need to stay project partners—that's it."

Natalie nodded, her expression thoughtful.

"Graduation *and* Luna do kind of put a stop to everything," she said sympathetically. "But good thing there's not much more that can happen in two weeks—unless there's another band contest somewhere."

I smiled a little, and while we talked about other things, I regretted the pink highlights I'd sprayed in my hair just that morning, as well as all the good things that had happened between Adam and I. The shift in our feelings had only been a cruel, unnatural trick, and the pain of saying goodbye to him soon made me wish our view of each other had never changed.

* * * * * *

My gaze lingered on Adam's empty desk the next morning as I waited for him in Reforming Literature. It seemed so silly now that he had sat in front of me for months this semester, yet neither of us had dared to say a word to each other until forced. To me, all that time felt needlessly wasted, and I wondered how differently things would have gone if I had tried to be a light sooner. But the sudden slap of Adam's backpack against his desk caused me to jump.

"We won the damn contest!" he exclaimed. "The results were posted this morning!"

My eyes widened while I stared into the excitement glowing from his face, but every nerve or feeling I had felt numb.

"Cool."

The word came out stale and cold, and I knew if today had been in the past, I would have hugged him for the first time—without a second thought.

"We won a *thousand* dollars," he urged, slightly confused. "This is amazing, Anna. Now we can make our demo as soon as we get to California."

My lips wouldn't move as I tried to force a smile, but when the bell rang, my gaze immediately dropped to my notebook. I could feel Adam's eyes on me before he sat down, and I tried to ignore the pain in my chest while Mr. Emery greeted the class, informing us that today would be the last work day before presentations started. I quickly decided to go to the library to avoid Adam, but as soon as Mr. Emery stopped talking, he turned to face me.

"Something wrong?" Adam asked, his brow furrowed.

I shook my head and stood, slipping on my backpack.

"Where are you going?" he continued.

"The library."

"Oh—I'll go with you."

"No," I snapped. "I want to work *alone* today."

Hurt and confusion spread across his face before I fled to Mr. Emery's desk for permission, then escaped into the hall. While I walked to the library, I took a deep, shaky breath—convinced I had done the right thing, despite how much I hated it.

Nothing would be different if we had talked sooner. Adam would still be going to California, and I'd still go to college this fall. We were always doomed.

I passed through the glass library doors less than a minute later, ignoring the table Adam and I had used when I chose one in the back of the main room. For a while, I tried working on one of the student laptops, but an endless stream of emotions made it impossible to focus. I purposely stayed in the library until class ended, and when I made it to Advanced 3D Art, I grabbed my *haute couture* showcase from a large storage cupboard and brought it to my desk. Two of the three mannequins were finished, but the third tie-dye dress needed a few more painted strips of newspaper. While I started to work, I felt a trickle of relief as my stress slowly disappeared.

Doesn't Adam realize everything between us is pointless? Maybe if I explained it to him, he'd understand completely, and not feel hurt...

The idea was only a little comforting, and once I finished the tie-dye dress, I stood up and stared proudly at the mannequins. The delicate paper feathers of the pink dress looked flashy and elegant, and the giant blue ruffles of the center dress were perfectly aligned and bouncy like I hoped. The tie-dye pattern of the last dress was clean and dramatic, and the small glass pieces I used instead of rhinestones sparkled beautifully. But the intensely satisfying moment shattered when my cell phone vibrated in my pocket, causing my heart to pound suddenly.

Adam?

I grabbed my phone and looked anxiously at the screen.

NATALIE: Remember Jake's friend Sean? He'll take you to prom.

My brow furrowed as memories of Sean from Jake's boat last summer faded into mind. I'd only seen him in passing a few times since, and although I never knew what he'd thought of me, I remembered thinking he was cute and somewhat funny.

ME: I do. Did he ask about me?

NATALIE: Well... we were talking about prom and I said you were looking for a date. He said he'd go with you.

I sighed heavily as I sagged down into my chair, filled with disappointment.

Clearly no one is going to ask me to prom. I guess I have to go with Sean now, because I have no good reason to go alone.

ME: Ok. I'll talk to him soon.

NATALIE: Great! We'll get a limo together :-)

I smiled a little, though I hardly felt happy.

I left the classroom with my showcase and carried it to the conference room near the library, where I saw other projects placed on top of the long table in the middle of the room. I chose an empty spot that faced away from the door and filled out a blank artist card, then propped it next to my mannequins. But as I walked toward the door, the urge to take a picture struck me, and I snapped a few photos on my cell phone before returning to class.

SPLIT | Adam

Thursday morning in Reform Lit, I still couldn't shake the terrible feeling Anna had given me two days ago. Even though I obsessively analyzed every second of our weekend together—which I thought was great—I couldn't figure out what I'd done wrong.

It's not me. Probably something else. No—it's definitely me.

Her silence behind me felt louder than anything else in the room while I sat at my desk, hardly paying attention to the first group that kicked off presentations.

Who cares why she's acting this way? If she doesn't want to talk about it—it's her problem.

I glared at the projector screen for most of the class period, the pain and confusion I felt killing my efforts to relax and let it go. When the bell rang an hour later, I immediately got up and slung my backpack over my shoulder, deciding not to confront her and make whatever I'd done worse. But I'd hardly taken a few steps before—

"Adam?"

I stopped, ignoring the urge to look at her in case I had hallucinated.

"Adam... I think we should talk."

My heart pounded as I turned around, realizing I hadn't imagined anything.

"Oh—um—sure," I replied.

Anna smiled a little and kept her gaze to the floor as I followed her out of the classroom into the crowded hallway. We were silent as we walked beside each other, but I had too many questions in my head to know what to say anyway. After turning into another hall, Anna led me inside an empty study room, where a table with chairs sat in front of a large window that looked out into a courtyard. I closed the door behind us and walked with her to the middle of the room, my stress almost doubling when I saw a few tears in her eyes.

"I know I've been acting weird," she admitted. "But everything is ending so quickly."

I furrowed my brow, unable to stop my hands from resting on her shoulders.

"What will all end soon? Do you have a brain tumor?"

Anna laughed a little, her eyes brightening.

"No—of course *not*. But our lives will be totally different after graduation, and what's the point of being friends if we're splitting up?"

"You're thinking too hard about this," I insisted. "Everything will be fine."

"Are you sure? I don't think I..."

"What?"

"Maybe I shouldn't have said friends."

My anxiety spiked as I stared her in the eye, the truth of my feelings practically exposed. But while Anna stared back without rejection or disgust, I started to realize she had exposed herself, too. The tense moment between us broke when the bell for next period rang, and Anna bit her lip while groaning in disappointment.

"Crap—I shouldn't have tried to do this right now," she said with a frown.

"Don't worry, I'm glad you did," I replied. "I thought you weren't talking to me because I did something to upset you."

Anna quickly shook her head.

"No—I'm sorry for making you feel bad. But, what about Luna? We can't act like she doesn't exist."

Guilt stabbed my gut, and I shrugged sluggishly.

"It's not like it was in the beginning," I said after a moment. "There's another side to her that I don't like—she can be pretty mean and jealous. Not to mention she doesn't think Lucid is good enough to be on our demo, when I thought she loved it. And she wants to live with us in California, but that's a lot more than me and the guys want to take on right now. I thought we had something great for a while, but I don't feel that serious about her anymore."

I sighed heavily while Anna nodded thoughtfully.

"Are you going to prom together?" she asked.

"Yeah."

"What happens after that, then? Are you breaking up with her?"

"I don't know. Her parents are making her wait until she turns eighteen in October to move to California, but I'm hoping she'll end it by then."

"You shouldn't wait," Anna insisted, her brow furrowed. "If you don't like her anymore, don't drag her feelings out. I wouldn't hope for her to magically change her mind."

I sighed, then groaned.

"Fine—I'll think of something. I just don't want to crush her."

"You already like someone else," Anna said quietly. "I think it's best to let her move on as soon as possible. You're really doing her a favor."

"Yeah, maybe. And I know it sucks that we won't see each other after graduation, but I think it's obvious ignoring me doesn't work."

Anna sighed, the corner of her mouth turning up slightly.

"You're right. The damage is already done."

I smiled and let go of her shoulders, hardly able to believe that I'd somehow won her over—though it sucked that time wasn't on our side. Anna tucked a strand of hair behind her ear as I sighed heavily.

"We should go to class," she added. "But Adam... I owe you something."

I raised a brow, waiting for her to say more. But Anna stepped toward me, her arms wrapping around my waist as she pressed the side of her face against my chest. My body felt stiff while surprise flooded me, but a few seconds later, I slid my arms around her and closed my eyes, soaking in her warm pressure.

"I should have said it sooner," Anna confessed lightly. "But congratulations winning the contest."

⬤ ⬤ ⬤ ⬤ ⬤ ⬤

Saturday night, I hung out at Nate's house with him, Dex, and Luna to officially celebrate winning the Screaming Rumble—something we still couldn't believe had happened while we drank beer on the back porch.

"Too bad you missed our best show ever," Dex teased Luna from across the outdoor table. "That night was incredible—once in a lifetime. We beat a ton of bands that have been around a lot longer."

Luna rolled her eyes and laughed.

"Once in a lifetime? I hope you haven't peaked yet," she replied. "But I *had* to go to my stupid cousin's wedding, or I would've been there."

Her plastic green chair sat beside mine as we faced Nate and Dex, but I hadn't said anything in a while, my thoughts constantly slipping to the memory of Anna's arms around me. Her touch had been innocent, but in the days and hours since, I kept imagining and wanting more.

I don't think she's had a boyfriend yet, which means she hasn't had—

Music blasting from Nate's phone brought me back to reality, and I realized the song was one of ours as I heard Dex's voice through the speakers.

"Someone recorded us at Loose Ella!" Nate shouted.

The three of us jumped from our seats and surrounded him, staring at the video of our performance on his cell screen. While the footage zoomed in and out, my heart pounded as I wondered if Anna might appear and enrage Luna, but thankfully the crowd stayed a giant black mass.

"Where did you find this?" Dex asked.

"On the club's website," Nate said. "They have a whole gallery of videos people uploaded."

While we watched, Luna crossed her arms and sighed heavily.

"I'm not waiting until I'm *eighteen* to move to Cali," she said heatedly. "I need to tell my parents I'm going after graduation whether they like it or not."

"Don't do that," I replied quickly. "We're still trying to figure things out right now."

"Like what? Steve wasn't a scammer, so you have an apartment now. *And* you just won the extra money you needed."

"It's not that simple. Trust me, okay?"

"Sure—whatever."

She frowned and went back to her chair while the urge to break up burned inside me. Despite Nate and Dex also being against her moving in with us, they didn't say anything, and I still hated the thought of confronting her. For the next few hours, we managed to talk about other things until I walked Luna to her car at midnight.

I need to call it quits now. It's mean to drag her feelings out, like Anna said. And we can't go to prom because that'll just make it worse.

"So… we need to talk about what's happening after graduation," I said, managing to sound calm while my blood raced.

Luna raised a brow as she looked at me with a narrow gaze.

"Good, because I've been trying too, and you keep saying nothing is figured out yet—which isn't true."

"Well, I didn't want to say it, but I've talked to the guys and we don't think you should move to California with us."

Luna groaned and rolled her eyes.

"Why? I'll get a job and everything will be okay," she insisted. "I don't care if I have to sleep on the couch or the floor. I don't want to go to college or anything like that—I just want to start a new life with you guys."

I stopped at the end of the driveway suddenly, causing Luna to take a step back and stare up at me.

"You can't come," I said, trying to keep my voice steady. "I'm sorry, but we want to do this on our own. And I… I really don't see us getting any more serious."

Luna's brown irises were almost as black as her eyeliner as her eyes widened in the dim street light.

"What does that mean?" she asked anxiously. "So what if we get annoyed with each other? That's how all couples are."

"It's more than that—I think we should break up."

She stared in shock before tears came into her eyes, and my stomach twisted as Luna pressed her face into her hands, which were covered by the long sleeves of her black sweater.

"What did I do?" she begged. "I know we haven't been getting along, but if you want to have sex—"

"No, that won't fix anything. You get angry and jealous a lot, and you said you loved Lucid when you didn't."

"I love it! I swear I do!"

"That's a lie! You said it wasn't good enough for our demo."

"I take it back, then. Please, put it on the demo. I love that song and—"

"I'm sorry Luna, but it's over, okay? We had our chance, but I'm moving away and I like someone else."

She sniffled a few times and caught her breath before her hands finally fell away from her face. I saw her eyeliner had streaked in several directions toward her cheeks, and although she looked upset, her eyes hardened.

"You like someone else? I bet I know who."

"It doesn't matter," I replied quickly. "I just wanted to be honest, because I have a lot of reasons for what I'm doing."

"Of course you do. Thanks a lot, Adam—you're the worst."

Luna turned and walked the rest of the way to her car parked along the curb, slamming the driver's door once she climbed inside. I watched as her tail lights disappeared quickly down the street, my chest heaving as my anxiety turned into relief.

PIECES | Anna

While I ate lunch alone on Monday, I felt lost in a spiral of grief and guilt. Despite my friendships with a few guys who could have asked me to prom, I felt crushed that *none* of them had—or likely would, at this point. And as much as I didn't want to go to prom with Sean, the only real reason I had to turn him down was my pride, which caused me to feel selfish and ungrateful.

I don't want a pity date, but why can't I get over it and be thankful for Natalie's help? If I don't go with Sean, then I'll have to sit at the table all night because I have no one to dance with, and that'll be boring and pathetic. I just have to accept that no one really wanted to go with me and make the best of it...

I sighed heavily as my gaze searched the cafeteria for Sean again, although I didn't know what lunch period he had. Natalie had switched her lunch periods that day for tutoring, however, I didn't mind processing all my thoughts and feelings alone at the moment. Eventually, I smiled a little as I remembered Sean on Jake's boat again last summer, and how hard he had made Natalie and I laugh while he danced ridiculously to the radio.

I shouldn't care so much how I got a date to prom because Sean's funny and we'll have a good time.

My smile widened while that thought satisfied me for the next few minutes, until I remembered something else—the surprise and happiness I saw on Jennifer McClellan's face in the parking lot yesterday, where someone had written 'Go to prom with me?' on her car windshield, along with leaving behind a card and bouquet of roses. My smile quickly faded as I replayed her excitement in my head, feeling the urge to disappear and never be seen again. Even though I didn't need an effort that extreme... there was nothing about going to prom with Sean that made me feel special.

Screw it—I won't go with him. God knows how much I want to be asked, and if no one will do it, then a date isn't meant for me.

I finished my lunch with a new sense of strength and independence, and left the cafeteria shortly afterward to head to my next class. But while I made my way through the crowd of students, I spotted Sean—as if by fate—standing in front of his locker. He stood tall with light brown hair and eyes, and his face had sharp angles, though his humorous personality kept his expression soft and friendly. Two of his friends were talking to him, and I stared at them while frozen in place.

There he is! Now tell him he can be my date!

I tried to take a step forward, but my newly formed strength and independence fought against me while flooding every atom of my being.

Why should I go to him? If he agreed to be my date, he can find me!

When my tense muscles relaxed, I passed by Sean and his friends a few seconds later, though it seemed he hadn't even noticed me. I felt confident that it was a sign as I walked the rest of the way to my Geometry class—glad that I would never be found.

* * * * * *

I tried to ignore the stares of my classmates as I walked toward the front of the room in Reform Lit Tuesday morning. Mr. Emery had chosen Adam and I to present our project first that day, and although it would take us less than twenty minutes, I still felt like an eternity would pass before I could safely retreat back to my desk. When I stood on the left side of the projector screen, I smiled awkwardly at Adam across from me, admiring his calm and nearly bored expression. He smiled back and held a small, black remote, which he used to turn on the ceiling-mounted projector once Mr. Emery had our presentation ready.

I took a deep breath when Adam clicked to the first slide and gave an overview of *Spiraled Life* before he spent the next few minutes explaining Stormer's childhood. Despite his normal talking speed and the five slides he clicked through, I hardly felt ready when it was suddenly my turn, and Adam held the remote out to me, grinning. My heart pounded as I took it from him, ignoring the class while I held a robotic-like stare on the projector screen. I tried to keep my voice steady as I started to explain Stormer's struggles with bulimia in her teen and adult years, though I finally relaxed a little as I clicked through a few slides. When it was Adam's turn again several minutes later, a wave of relief passed through me as I happily handed the remote back to him, then listened while he ended the presentation with Stormer's transformed self-image and recovery.

While the class clapped afterward, I quickly escaped back to my seat, my nerves still on edge as the next partner group went to the front of the class. During their presentation, my thoughts gradually drifted to my showcase, which had been on display for a week now. Although it was possible Adam had already seen it, he hadn't said a word about it, and I grew excited as I thought about asking him after class. But the next forty-five minutes were torture until the bell finally rang, and I immediately tapped Adam on the shoulder.

"Have you seen my showcase yet?" I asked him quickly. "It's been in the conference room by the library for a week."

He shook his head, sliding his backpack over his shoulder.

"No. How'd the *hot coucher* turn out?"

"What?" I asked with a laugh. "It's *haute couture*."

"Oh—that word is too fancy for normal people."

"No, it's not. You just need practice," I replied. "Want to see it real quick?"

"Yeah, let's go."

I stood and pulled my backpack over my shoulder, then walked with Adam into the hall. But less than a minute passed before he took a deep breath and ran a hand through his hair.

"So... I broke up with Luna on Saturday," he said calmly.

"Seriously? How did that happen?"

"I just told her all the reasons it wasn't working anymore," he replied confidently. "And, well—I admitted to liking you, too."

"Oh... what did she say?"

"Not much. She just said I was the worst before leaving Nate's house."

"Wow. I'm sorry. How do you feel?"

"Fine, honestly. I'm glad I'm not dragging things out anymore."

"Yeah. I bet it was hard, but you made the right choice."

"Definitely."

I smiled a little, though I had no romantic experience to compare it to. While we walked toward the conference room, I glanced down at Adam's hand when it bumped into mine, but I ignored an urge to lace my fingers through his.

He's single now, but still not my boyfriend.

The conference room was empty when we reached it a minute later, and I led Adam around the long table in the middle toward my mannequin showcase on the opposite side. I was already smiling as we approached it and overly excited to explain my inspiration for each piece—but what I saw instead of my finished project turned my reality into a sudden nightmare. The

Styrofoam body of each mannequin was broken into countless pieces around the wooden platform, and the painted newspaper of each dress laid torn and scattered across the table top. I stared at the destruction of my showcase in utter shock, hardly able to believe it had been destroyed beyond repair or recognition. Tears fell from my eyes as I stared down at it, overwhelmed by floods of pain and confusion.

"What the hell *happened?*" I heard Adam say with alarm. "Who *did* this?"

My arms felt numb as I reached out and held a few pieces of broken Styrofoam in my hands.

"When did this happen?" Adam continued frantically.

"I—I don't know," I replied. "I just saw my showcase yesterday morning. Everything was fine—it wasn't broken, then—"

I couldn't stop staring at the broken pieces in horror until I found myself suddenly facing Adam, his grip tight on my shoulders. His thick eyebrows were furrowed with concern, and the unsettled look in his eyes matched my own.

"Who would do this?" he asked.

"I don't know. Maybe—maybe it was an accident."

"You're not going to class, are you?"

"No," I replied, shaking my head. "I can't think about anything else right now. I worked so hard on this, Adam, and you never got to see—"

Tears slid down my hot cheeks again, and within seconds, Adam pulled me against him, his arms tight around me. The side of my face rested on his chest while I hugged his waist and let go of the Styrofoam pieces I held.

"Go home and relax," he insisted, his voice low. "We'll figure out what happened."

"Okay. I just want to be alone for a while."

Adam nodded, but neither of us moved. I closed my eyes and took a deep breath, enjoying the unexpected comfort of his warmth.

⁂

"It will be okay, Anna. I'm sure your teacher will understand."

My mother sat on the edge of my bed while I laid beneath the covers later that night, my eyes locked on my cell phone screen. I stared at the picture I'd taken of my showcase a week ago, which turned out to be a happy surprise that I remembered once I'd gotten home. I sighed and lowered my arm as I looked at her.

"I hope so, and I'm so glad I took a picture of it. But how did it get destroyed? It has to be an accident somehow, right?"

My mother frowned and shrugged.

"I don't know, but if I were to guess based on how you described it... that doesn't sound like an accident."

"No one would do that on purpose! I haven't done anything bad to anyone."

"I know—I wish I had the answer. But I'm glad Adam was nice to you about it."

I smiled, my mood shifting more positively.

"Yeah, he helped a lot, and you were right about him. He's changed a lot since he's gotten to know me, and I've changed, too. He actually just broke up with—"

My eyes widened suddenly as my whole body stiffened. Although I had never done anything to intentionally hurt someone, I finally realized there was a person who probably hated me at Gainesville High.

Luna... she did it!

FIX | Adam

For the rest of the day, I couldn't forget how Anna looked when she saw her project was destroyed. It crushed me to see tears in her eyes, and I wished I could have done a lot more to fix the problem than just hugging her. But whoever wrecked her showcase had ruined it beyond fixing, and as I walked across the parking lot after school, I couldn't ignore the nagging feeling in my gut that told me who'd done it.

Luna did this! She hates Anna, and obviously wanted revenge. But if she's going to play dirty, then she's going to pay for it, too.

I yanked open the driver's door of my Thunderbird and climbed inside, hoping Dex could help me figure out the truth, as well as how to pay Luna back if she had any part in it. The drive to his house took less than ten minutes, and after I parked on the curb and shut off my blaring music, I jogged through the yard to his front door. When I knocked, Dex answered a minute later.

"You look terrible," I said flatly.

"Really? I'm not actually sick today."

"I know—liar."

Dex shoved my shoulder while I smirked, then motioned me inside.

"Guess what? Someone destroyed Anna's showcase today."

My mood quickly shifted as anger-fueled heat covered my body, and Dex furrowed his eyebrows.

"What? I need more details than that, man."

"She worked on an art project for weeks that someone tore to pieces... but I'm sure I know who did it."

Dex still looked confused, but after a minute, he nodded.

"Oh—I get it. You think Luna did it?"

"I know she did. Who else?"

"Let me text Chelsea," Dex replied, pulling his cell from his pocket. "She'll know if Luna did it, or she'll find out."

I waited anxiously while he typed a text and sent it, but then put his cell back in his pocket.

"You must've told Luna you liked Anna?"

"Yeah, I did."

"Damn—bringing up someone else during a break up is brutal."

"Well, I told her all my reasons. I wanted her to know that I meant it, because she didn't want to break up or stay in Florida."

"I guess you did what you had to do, but it's too bad Anna got sucker punched, so to speak."

"I know. But if Luna did it, she's going to pay for it."

Dex's cell made a noise and he took it back out of his pocket, staring at the screen.

"Chelsea doesn't know anything," he replied, disappointed. "But she says to text Amber because she and Luna are in a fight. She'll probably snitch on her."

I grinned while he typed another text to Amber, and afterward, we walked through the one-story house to his bedroom in the back. Dex's room had dark blue walls and a large window covered by black curtains next to his bed, and along with a messy closet, he had an old dresser that held his flat screen and game console.

"You really want to date a church girl?" he asked, picking up two controllers from the floor. "I mean, I know Anna is cool enough to see our show, but still... she's a whole different breed from us."

I shrugged as I walked to the end of his bed and sat on it.

"I'm not going to date her, Dex. We're going to California, remember?"

"You don't want to try anyway?"

"No. It would be too complicated, and long distance sucks."

"Yeah. You can't make out with her."

He smirked as he sat next to me, putting a controller in my lap.

"I can hardly imagine kissing her. Even though she likes me, it still seems impossible."

"If you had more time, maybe you'd get further than that."

Dex pressed a button in the middle of his controller to turn on the gaming console, and though I tried to imagine going even further than a kiss with Anna—my brain still couldn't handle it.

I need to be alone so I can focus, then maybe... I can picture it all...

Dex's cell made another noise, and my blood suddenly raced as he checked his phone again, though this time, he quickly smiled.

"It's Amber," he said excitedly. "Luna *did do it.* She was talking about it at lunch on Monday."

"What should we do to her then?" I asked angrily. "Maybe ruin something of hers?"

Dex stared at the floor while he thought for a minute, then laughed.

"Does she keep her car locked? What if you smeared paint on her seats?"

"What?"

"Come on, man—it's called poetic justice. She ruined Anna's art project, so now her seats get ruined with paint."

I raised a brow as I considered it, knowing I could easily buy some black paint at the store that afternoon to stain her tan seats.

"You're a genius! She doesn't lock her car that much, so it's a perfect plan."

"Of course it is, but don't get busted doing it," he said, mostly joking. "Ready to nuke some aliens now?"

Without an answer, Dex started our game from the menu screen, and while we played, I realized I had never felt so impatient to go back to school.

* * * * * *

After the first lunch period the next day, I texted Anna to meet me outside the cafeteria. I could hardly wait to see her again and explain the payback I had planned, but when I saw her, the sadness in her face killed some of my excitement.

"How's it going?" I asked gently.

"It's okay," she replied with a shrug. "What did you want to tell me?"

"Well—I found out who ruined your project. It definitely wasn't an accident. Maybe you won't believe it, but... it was Luna."

Anna raised her eyebrows, though she surprised me with a nod.

"Last night... I thought she might have done it," she confessed, biting her lip. "I remembered how you told me that she knew you liked me, and... it made sense."

"Yeah, it makes a lot of sense, but don't worry—she's not getting away with it," I insisted. "I'm going to smear paint inside her car today."

The sadness in Anna's face suddenly shifted to shock and worry.

"What? Adam! You can't do *that*. You'll get arrested!"

"No, I won't! There's no cameras in the parking lot."

Anna frowned, her eyes suddenly growing frightened after she gazed past my shoulder.

"We need to leave," she said anxiously.

I furrowed my brow and turned, my whole body tensing as I saw Luna walking down the hall with three of her friends. My expression hardened while

I glared at her, and when she noticed us, her face immediately twisted into disgust. Anna didn't make a sound as I stared at them, expecting Luna and her pack to ignore us in hateful silence as they walked into the cafeteria—but a girl with short black hair and a nose ring stopped a short distance in front of us.

"You ruined her life!" she shouted, her gaze flashing between me and Anna.

I laughed mockingly and looked back at Anna, whose face was more pale than before.

"That's—that's *not* true," she managed, her voice hardly loud enough for them to hear.

"Cheater and boyfriend-stealer!" another friend yelled.

"So that's what you think?" I snapped back. "For the record, you have *no* idea—"

"You *tore* my project to PIECES!"

My heart pounded in surprise when Anna unexpectedly shouted, and I saw the paleness of her face had morphed into a red fury. Her heated gaze was fixed solely on Luna, and my shock increased when she took a step toward the group—causing me to instinctively grab her wrist.

What the hell—is Anna going to fight?

"Who cares! You're a religious freak!" Luna finally erupted, breaking her silence. "I lost *everything I wanted* because of you!"

Her friends started insulting us again, but a middle-aged lunch aide came out of the cafeteria, her irritated gaze shifting between us and Luna's group.

"What's going on out here?" she demanded.

A long silence dragged while none of us said a word, and the lunch aide motioned Luna and her friends forward.

"If you're coming to lunch, get in line now," she instructed.

The girls didn't look at us as they quickly walked into the cafeteria, and afterward, the lunch aide looked at me and Anna.

"You can go in a minute. I suggest you give them some space."

The older lady turned and went back into the cafeteria, and when I looked at Anna, I remembered my hand around her wrist and let it go.

"You alright?" I asked, worried.

"Fine," she replied stiffly.

"You sure? I thought you might take Luna down."

Anna's red face faded into its normal color when she smiled.

"What? I'd never do that."

"Good, because you don't need to do anything—I've already got her payback handled."

Anna sighed and shook her head.

"No, Adam. Luna will *know* it was you and I don't want to repeat what just happened, okay?"

She gazed into my eyes desperately, but I couldn't stop myself from frowning.

"Please, let it go," she insisted. "I appreciate what you're trying to do for me, but my teacher understands and my grade won't be affected."

I shrugged in final defeat and rolled my eyes.

"Fine—I won't do it, I guess, and I'm glad your teacher is cool about it. But... meet me at my car after school, okay?"

Anna raised a brow, the corner of her mouth turning with a small smile.

"Why?"

I smiled at her, too.

"Well, I just thought of something else that'll make this whole thing a lot better."

● ● ● ● ● ●

I rushed out of the building when school ended and walked alone toward my car on the far side of the senior parking lot. After tossing my backpack in the passenger seat, I opened the center console and pulled out the prom tickets I'd bought a few weeks ago, then slid them into my pocket.

Why didn't I put more thought into this? What if she already has a date?

I closed the driver's door and walked to the back of the Thunderbird, leaning against the trunk while I watched other students climb into their cars and leave. I scanned every face as I looked for Anna, hoping that she wouldn't be put off by my spur-of-the-moment idea I'd hinted at earlier. But when I saw her break from the crowd a few minutes later, my anxiety started turning into calm excitement.

"Hi, Adam," Anna said, stopping in front of me. "What's going on?"

"Hey. How much do you trust me?"

"Um... a lot, I guess."

"Good. I wish I could fix your project for you, but since I can't... close your eyes and hold out your hand."

Anna raised a brow as she looked at me in confusion, but seconds later, she closed her eyes and lifted her palm. I reached into my pocket and took out the prom tickets, placing them gently in her hand. Anna's fingers curled around them, but she didn't open her eyes.

"Will you be my date to prom?"

Anna gasped as her eyes opened and she stared at the prom tickets, holding them in front of her face like they were made of gold.

"Maybe you have a date already, but—"

She threw her body suddenly into mine as she wrapped her arms around my neck and squealed happily in my ear.

"Yes, Adam! I'm not going with anyone else!"

My hands locked on her hips while she squirmed against me and squealed again, causing my grin to spread from ear to ear in victory. Despite my last minute plan to make her feel better, Anna seemed no less happy than Jennifer McClellan two days ago with a lot more pomp and circumstance.

"You have no idea how much this means to me," she said in relief. "I almost decided to go with someone else, but he didn't even ask, or care."

"What? You serious?"

"Yes."

Anna pulled back, her nose and lips only a few inches from mine. While I stared into her gray eyes, I forgot everything around us as I studied them, deciding not to kiss her—yet.

"You know, I do have one condition."
Her eyes widened a little.
"Look hot for me, okay?" I asked.
Anna rolled her eyes and smirked.
"Back at you, mister."

PROM | Anna

A few minutes before Adam pulled into the driveway late Saturday afternoon, I stood waiting for him on the front porch of my parent's house. I wore a loose button-up t-shirt and shorts, and my hair was curled and pinned back from my hair appointment earlier that day. Adam climbed out of his car and walked toward me with a plastic garment bag over his arm—a strange sight that led to a stranger thought of seeing him in a dress shirt and slacks later that night.

"You look great," Adam said, climbing the porch steps. "I like your prom outfit."

"I'm not wearing this!" I replied with a laugh. "I made my own dress, remember?"

"Of course. I like your hair, too."

Adam wrapped his finger in a loose strand of hair around my face, and my cheeks immediately started to burn.

"How are you with parents?" I asked anxiously. "Mine want to meet you, and they're right inside—"

"I'm fine with parents," he said coolly. "I have some, you know."

"True, but this is different."

"Do you like your parents?"

"Yes, but... I've never had a boyfriend, or even a date. I'm not sure how this will go."

Adam shrugged.

"Don't worry about it—let's go in."

I sighed, nodding once before I turned toward the front door. We walked into the foyer and I led Adam into the kitchen, where my dad was busy loading the dishwasher while my mom sat at the dining table, looking at her cell phone. Both of them gazed at us when Adam and I entered, and a brief, awkward silence passed.

"Hi, Adam," my dad said in a friendly tone. "We've heard a lot about you."

"Oh, no," he replied, joking. "What did Anna say?"

"Only good things—lately," I replied quickly, smiling.

My mom laughed and set her phone down on the dining table.

"It's nice to meet you," she said. "Dave, want to teach them the waltz?"

"Of course," he said happily. "I happen to be the only expert in Gainesville."

"No—we don't need to learn *the waltz*," I replied, annoyed. "We're going upstairs now, okay?"

My parents smiled as we left them, and Adam followed me up the staircase beside the foyer to the second floor. I opened the bathroom door on the left and motioned him inside, then pointed to the toilet lid.

"Take a seat," I said, smirking. "You're getting your hair done, too."

Adam stared at me from the doorway, his eyes widening.

"What? Aren't fancy clothes enough?"

"That's only the beginning," I replied. "Remember how I changed for Loose Ella? You need to look like the perfect gentlemen tonight."

Adam sighed, putting his garment bag on the counter before he sat on the toilet lid. I opened the drawer next to the sink and grabbed a black comb and a tube of hair gel, trying not to look too excited while I squeezed a thick line of gel across the teeth of the comb. Adam rested his chin on his fist, his pouting as plain as my joy.

"Don't worry! I promise you'll look great."

"I don't care," he grumbled. "I just—I need to smoke, but haven't been able to lately."

"Why?"

"I always feel weird about it, or my body acts strange. Maybe the universe wants me to quit."

For a long moment, I stared at him in shock, then laughed.

"The universe? Please, it was *me!* I've been praying for you to stop."

"What? Are you serious?"

"Yes! You said to pray that you wouldn't get lung cancer after the field trip, so, I've been praying for you to quit."

Shock spread across Adam's face while I grinned.

"See? God is *real,*" I continued. "If you don't try to smoke again, my prayers will work completely."

Adam raised a brow, though he said nothing. I kept smiling as I combed his hair, untangling the long locks and smoothing them out evenly with the gel. Adam sat silently while I parted his hair to one side and swept the ends of it toward the back of his head, each piece laying perfectly in place with little effort. When I finished a few minutes later, I stepped back and admired my work.

"Ready to see it? I *love* it."

Adam stepped in front of the mirror quickly and gripped the edge of the counter top, studying his polished hairdo carefully.

"Not bad," he admitted at length. "You really want me to be a pretty boy, don't you?"

"Maybe a little," I replied, half-joking. "But definitely tonight. You should model instead of making music."

Adam rolled his eyes with a mocking laugh.

"Sure, but what's next, then? Are you shaving my armpits?"

I gasped dramatically, my nose wrinkling.

"Absolutely *not.* Get dressed and meet me downstairs in a few minutes, okay?"

* * * * * *

I secretly admired Adam while I watched him from the top of the staircase. I could hardly believe how God had answered my prayer through someone I used to find detestable—but tonight, Adam looked so heavenly.

Along with his gelled hair, he was stunning in his maroon dress shirt and black suspenders, as well as his long black slacks and shiny shoes. He stood patiently with his hands in his pockets, and as I started down the stairs, he looked up at me.

I smiled, my gaze shifting to the steps below me as I carefully made my way down to the foyer, where Adam met me at the bottom of the switchback staircase. I stood one step higher than him while he studied my prom dress, and I sensed that his impression of me went as deeply as mine toward him.

"You're beautiful," he said quietly after a long moment.

"You're perfect," I whispered back.

My gaze drifted to his lips, and I instinctively closed my eyes, hoping Adam would lean in and kiss me. But—

"Ready to go to the park? You both look so wonderful and grown up!"

My body tensed at the sudden sound of my mother's voice, and I nodded, my cheeks burning with embarrassment. Adam appeared undisturbed, and very possibly unaware of what I'd imagined in the nanosecond before my mother's interruption. We left the house with my parents and climbed into my dad's SUV before driving fifteen minutes to Greenwood Park, where we had agreed to meet Natalie, Jake, their parents, and Adam's mom at six-thirty. There, everyone except Adam's mom waited on the grass next to the parking lot, and after I climbed out of the SUV, Natalie and I ran toward each other, hugging.

"I love your dress!" Natalie said. "You're so talented!"

Her blonde hair was pinned back into a curly, messy bun, and she wore a strapless dress made of blueish-gray satin fabric, along with a navy sash that tied around her waist. Jake stood nearby, the color of his dress shirt matching her gown like Adam's matched mine, and he also wore suspenders, black slacks, and shiny shoes.

"Thanks! You look wonderful!" I gushed.

The sound of tires rolling across gravel nearby caused me to turn, and I saw Adam walk toward a red car that was parked next to my dad's SUV. My stomach whirled with butterflies as I saw his mother through the windshield, and when she climbed out, she happily looked him over before hugging him. I took a deep breath and slowly walked toward them, but Adam's mother noticed me immediately and smiled.

"Anna! It's great to meet you," she said, her tone friendly. "You look wonderful, and so does Adam. I've never seen him like this!"

I smiled shyly and laughed.

"He didn't want his hair combed," I confessed. "But it adds the perfect touch."

We then walked toward everyone else, and once the parents were acquainted, our group traveled across the grass to the small lake at the back of the park. The scenery was beautiful with weeping willows and flower gardens, and Natalie and I stood in front of Jake and Adam while we posed for our parent's cameras. The photo shoot lasted until our white limousine arrived ten minutes later, its long body distantly visible in the parking lot. After we all made our way to it, the four of us said goodbye to our parents and greeted the limo driver, who held the rear door open for us.

Jake and Natalie were the first to climb in, taking the short row of seats across the back of the private cabin. I followed behind them into the entirely black space, and chose the closest seat along the left side, which had enough spots to sit seven people. Music played at a comfortable volume through the ceiling speakers, and lines of small, individual lights lit the edges of the floor and ceiling. When Adam joined me seconds later, the sides of our bodies pressed together as he put his arm around my shoulders, and my face warmed with satisfaction—convinced I had passed from the normal world and into a flawless dream.

"We should go everywhere like this!" Natalie said, overcome like I was.

"I know," I replied with a laugh. "We need to get rich!"

"I could get used to this," Adam added thoughtfully. "But where's the champagne?"

"No kidding," Jake said, his tone serious. "I'd say the occasion calls for it."

We talked and joked for the next thirty minutes while the limo drove us to the Romara Botanical Gardens, where our prom was being held at their event hall. When it stopped in front of a large, white brick building, we waited for the driver to open our door again before we stepped out onto the gravel driveway. Adam offered me his hand while I climbed out last from the private compartment, and I gratefully took it, lifting the hem of my dress with my other free hand. A narrow sidewalk led from the driveway to the cement steps of the event hall, which had open double doors and was mostly covered by vines with beautiful blooming flowers. While the four of us walked down the sidewalk, I sighed in admiration at the colorful flower beds as well as the glowing lanterns that hung from short metal poles around us.

"It's all so amazing, isn't it?" Adam said quietly.

Surprised, I looked at him, nodding.

"I felt like I was living a dream when we were in the limo," I confessed. "I'm glad that feeling hasn't changed."

Adam smiled a little, his hand squeezing mine for a moment.

"Tonight is already a lot better than I imagined. I'm glad I'm here with you."

I looked away, trying to hide my ridiculous grin.

"Me too, Adam."

We climbed the cement steps behind Natalie and Jake into the open double doors of the event hall, giving our tickets to an adult sitting behind a table inside the small front room. The four of us then walked through another pair of open doors into the formal dance hall, where the stunning glass ceiling showed the pinkish-orange sky transitioning slowly into a dark blue. The round tables that filled the front half of the dance hall were covered in white cloth and sprinkled with different colored flower petals, along with one glowing lantern resting in the center. The furthest half of the room held the dance floor, DJ booth, and buffet, and strings of light were draped across the ceiling around two beautiful vintage chandeliers. Although most of the senior class had already arrived, I found it hard to pay attention to anyone else as I felt entranced by all the charming details around me.

"What should we do?" I heard Natale ask. "Do you guys want to eat first, or should we dance...?"

"Let's eat," Jake replied. "The food smells great over there."

Without hesitation, the three of us followed him to the buffet line, but Natalie soon pulled me aside.

"I just want to say that I'm so glad you're here with Adam instead of Sean," she whispered happily. "Thank God he asked right in the nick of time!"

"I know! It was an incredible moment," I said, holding her hands. "Even though we don't have a lot of time left, tonight will be one of my greatest memories."

"Without a doubt, but I'm sure you'll see Adam again after graduation. You just have to keep in touch."

"We will," I replied confidently. "And you win—I like him a lot."

Natalie hugged me and we returned to Adam and Jake, who were already busy making jokes about a mainstream band. Fortunately, the buffet line moved quickly, and we claimed an empty table ten minutes later with plates full of delicious food. But while Natalie, Jake, and Adam did most of the talking, my gaze lingered on the crowd of couples who swayed slowly on the dance floor. My heart pounded at the thought of resting against Adam with his arms around me, fully relaxed and in awe of each other—much unlike when he'd tried to comfort me not long ago, after the horror of finding my art project destroyed. But those memories disappeared quickly, however, for there was one thing even more unimaginable that caused my blood to race.

Will Adam kiss me tonight? If I'm truly living inside a dream, then I just have to wait, even if it's the wonderful moment right before I wake up—

The gentle touch of Adam's hand just above my knee caused my thoughts to vanish. I looked at him with a shy smile, uncertain of the current conversation between him, Natalie, and Jake.

"Do you want to?" he asked, his eyebrows raised.

"Do I want to... what?"

"Dance," he said with a laugh. "Jake and Natalie are ready to go to the dance floor."

"Oh—of course."

I rose from my chair with Adam, and he took my hand as we walked toward the swaying couples, leading me toward an empty corner of the dance floor. When I faced him a minute later, I wrapped my arms loosely around his neck, and his hands settled comfortably above my hips. I sighed quietly and rested the side of my face against his shoulder, closing my eyes while the slow music created a heavenly atmosphere. Although I could hardly imagine a more perfect moment between us—save for a kiss—I was surprised Adam had gone this far into the evening without a complaint, and instead, seemed to easily submit to its possibly awkward expectations.

He's doing it for me... and for him. He's just as captivated as I am with this place. But if we kiss, I don't want it to happen in here...

I lifted my head and looked at Adam, but instead of meeting his gaze right away, his eyes stayed closed for a few long seconds.

"Dreaming?" I asked with a small smile.

"Yeah—dreaming within a dream. Is that possible?"

"I think so. I hope I didn't ruin it."

"No, you're still in front of me."

His relaxed hold on my waist tightened slightly, and I stared into his eyes, my thumb stroking his cheek while I cupped the side of his face.

"Want to take a walk?" I asked quietly.

"Why, and where?"

"Come on."

I took Adam's hand and pulled away from him, leading him back toward the double doors that led out to the front of the building. The adult who took our tickets earlier had disappeared, and we left the event hall without being noticed, following another path that led around the left side of the building at the bottom of the cement steps. When Adam and I made the turn, I smiled pleasantly as I saw the path would lead us deeper into the dark, extensive gardens beyond the event hall.

"What's your plan?" Adam asked calmly.

"Plan?" I countered innocently. "There is none."

"Sure. Whatever we can do alone out here, we can do back in there, right?"

I grinned slyly at him, and we walked in silence past more beautiful flower beds and countless solar lights that lit our way. Ahead, two curving lines of hedgerows trailed either side of the cement path, and at the end of it, I could faintly see a white bridge arching over a narrow creek.

"Maybe I do have a plan," I finally confessed. "I'll tell you on the white bridge."

Adam raised a brow as he glanced at me, but said nothing, and we reached the white bridge a few minutes later. It creaked slightly beneath our weight while we stood in the middle of it, and despite no longer having solar lights around us, the moonlight shined brightly enough to see Adam's handsome face.

"There's something I want to do," I said, my hands resting in his. "But not on the dance floor—it just wasn't private enough."

"I think I know," Adam replied, his tone satisfied. "This spot is much better by a long shot."

"It is. But I don't... how do we..."

"Don't think—just close your eyes."

I took a deep breath and closed them, my pulse quickening as Adam's lips pressed into mine. My fingers curled around his suspenders while sensations I'd never felt before flowed throughout my body, and Adam increased the pressure of his mouth before his lips parted slightly. I tilted my head back to let my bottom lip slide between both of his, and my hands cupped the sides of his face while our mouths met and separated in rhythm with our need for air. But it seemed less than a few minutes had passed before an alarm went off inside me, and I pushed Adam back, though nearly intoxicated from the most physical pleasure I'd ever felt.

"That was perfect," I replied, bathed in warmth. "But it was enough."

"Yeah? You sure?"

"Yes, but... I could never imagine a better first kiss."

"Terrific—I was just getting started."

My eyes widened as I stared into his, wondering just how deep the pleasure could go between us.

"I bet you and Luna kissed a lot?"

"Sometimes."

Adam's brow furrowed as if he felt uncomfortable, and I easily dropped the subject.

"We should go back," I said unhappily. "I'm sure Natalie and Jake are wondering where we are."

"Probably... but I don't want to."

"Me either."

We stared into each other's eyes again, and I smiled little, rising on my toes to kiss him sweetly.

"I'll never forget tonight," I told him. "You have no idea how magical everything has been for me."

"I feel it too," he replied, taking my hand. "Let's go back and finish our dance."

Three words I didn't expect suddenly came to mind as my heart melted, but I walked wordlessly beside him off the white bridge with our fingers laced.

MEMORY | Adam

The night before graduation felt bittersweet as I climbed in my car around six on Friday to pick up Anna and take her to one of my favorite spots in town. Even though I couldn't wait to start my road trip with the guys to California after the ceremony tomorrow, it was hard not knowing when I'd see Anna again.

While I drove down the street, I thought about our first kiss on the white bridge like I had all week, and how I'd truly felt the magic she'd mentioned in all of it—her lips, the moonlight, the gardens, our dance—everything. But as great as it had been, there was an important piece we would miss, though sex with Anna was never a real possibility in the short amount of time we had. And it didn't take much to believe that sleeping with her would be a lot better than my first experience or any other I'd had with Luna—mainly because once the excitement wore off, I hardly felt a real connection to her. I sighed heavily, forcing myself to think of something else.

A lot of people believe in God, and maybe he's real since Anna's prayers got me to quit smoking. But why would some cosmic being care about my stupid problems?

I furrowed my brow as I braked at a stop sign, unable to make sense of it as I turned onto a street near Anna's subdivision.

I guess there's only one way to really know. If I go to California and make millions off my music, then I'll believe in God, too.

Despite my honest bet, I smirked and followed a long street to where Anna's house sat near the end of a cul-de-sac. I saw her waiting on the porch for me like she had last Saturday, and she wore a purple tank top and shorts, along with a crossbody purse. While I pulled next to the curb, she started across the lawn, pulling open the passenger door a minute later. After she slid down inside and clicked her seat belt, Anna smiled at me.

"You've been waiting there all day for me, haven't you?" I asked, teasing.

"Please," she replied with an eye roll. "I was only outside for a few minutes."

"Sure—you're addicted to me."

Anna raised a brow as I grinned, and I circled my car around out of the cul-de-sac. While we left the back streets of the subdivision, Anna opened her purse and pulled out a CD case, which I analyzed in a single glance. The front of it showed three illustrated men that looked like priests, but I knew enough about them to get the joke.

"Why the hell do you have that?" I asked curiously. "Don't you know they're not really *God's favorite band?*"

"Of course! But some of their songs are really good. Do you like them?"

I shrugged. "Mainstream, but not terrible."

When Anna ejected one of my CD's from the center dash, I jumped in my seat.

"Hey! I control the music!"

"Chill! Just listen, okay?"

Anna pushed her CD in and skipped ahead a few tracks, then turned up the volume. A snare drum solo blasted through the speakers, which was soon followed by an electric guitar riff before vocals. Anna reached inside her purse again, taking out two pens that she drummed against the glove box while singing loudly along with the lyrics. I stared at her in shock—hardly able to remember when I'd felt so amazed, terrified, and confused all at once.

"Sing with me!" she shouted.

Her demand broke my brain freeze, and I started singing at the top of my lungs while we drove across town, the amplified bass in my car causing it to vibrate like crazy. But when the song ended, Anna turned off the CD player while we tried to catch our breath.

"So... what do you... think of me... now?" she asked.

"What does... that mean?"

"I'm not some... *innocent* church girl... am I?"

I shrugged a little. "You're just... a fraction less... now."

We were silent for several long seconds until our breathing returned to normal, and Anna furrowed her eyebrows as she stared out the windshield.

"Will you tell me where we're going yet?"

"Nope, but we're almost there."

We headed toward a few large hills just outside of town, and when we reached the paved road that led into them, we passed a polished boulder that read *Wyndemere Hills*. Anna's mouth fell open in a silent gasp when she saw it, and I tried to pretend like I didn't notice her expression, or the fancy boulder.

"Wyndemere Hills?" she said in awe. "Do you know someone who lives here?"

"No, but we won't bother anyone," I replied casually. "Wait until we get to the top."

The hidden, ritzy subdivision overlooked the town, and we drove by many houses with private gates, pools, and multi-car garages, as well as the occasional water fountain. After ten minutes, I turned right into a gravel turnaround and parked at the top of the highest hill, which gradually sloped into the backyard of one of the mansions below. The whole city of Gainesville was spread out through my windshield, and a stunning mix of pink, orange, and yellow filled the evening sky.

"See why I like to come here?" I said, shutting off the engine.

Anna nodded, her eyes locked on the view.

"Yeah... this place is incredible."

"Come on, let's sit on the hood."

After popping the trunk, I climbed out of my car and grabbed a large, thick blanket from it, then threw the blanket over the hood of the Thunderbird. Anna stood on the other side and watched me, her brow raised as she looked uncertain. I smiled, motioning to her as I climbed onto the hood. Anna waited a few seconds before she finally joined me, the side of her body pressing against mine while I wrapped my arm around her shoulders.

"Are you sure the hood will hold us?" she asked.

"It's holding us now," I replied. "Don't worry."

She smiled a little, and we gazed at the town and sky silently for a while.

"You know... I've been thinking about fashion school," Anna said quietly. "But I haven't told anyone."

"That's great. Are you going?"

"I don't know, but I'd like to. I'm still going to study accounting this fall, but if that doesn't work out for some reason, then... maybe I'll go to fashion school instead."

"You should do it. Don't listen to anyone else."

"Much easier said than done," she replied.

"Yeah, but you love it, and that means something. I can't believe how amazing your drawings are, or that you actually *made* your prom dress. I'm still impressed by how incredible it was."

"It wasn't bad for a ten dollar pattern," Anna replied, half-joking. "But I did add some personal touches. I'm going to keep that dress for a long time."

"Definitely. Even though I've written a lot of trash songs, I'm never getting rid of my notebooks."

Anna's eyes brightened.

"Good! Maybe something you've written will pop out at you again."

I shrugged and we gazed back at Gainesville, but this time, I struggled to enjoy the sunset. Despite it being beautiful, the sun seemed to be sinking too quickly, and I couldn't ignore that in less than twelve hours, graduation would finally separate us. I sighed heavily as I stared at the town, and Anna pulled her knees up, wrapping her arms around her legs. After glancing at her, I thought she looked depressed, and I wondered if the same thing had crossed her mind right then.

"We're going to talk every day, right?" she asked sadly.

"Of course," I replied, trying to sound casual. "We'll text every day and talk a lot on the phone."

"You're leaving after the ceremony ends?"

"Yeah... we already have everything packed in the van. But I'm not leaving until I say goodbye."

A muscle in my jaw tightened while I dreaded the moment, but Anna continued staring at Gainesville, her expression thoughtful.

"We should say goodbye tonight," she suggested. "Everything is so wonderful right now... it would be the perfect memory."

"You sure?"

"Yes. We're going to be so busy tomorrow, and I'd rather not think about it then."

"Okay."

Anna turned her face toward me, but her eyes were closed. She tilted her head back to raise her lips, and without hesitation, I leaned into her. The smaller size of her mouth fit perfectly with mine, and while our kissing intensified, Anna lowered herself down against the blanket. I focused on the quiet sounds she made while my top half covered her, and I liked the gentle touch of her fingertips along my jaw and neck. But just when I started to deepen the kiss—to feel with my tongue between her teeth—Anna pushed back against my shoulders.

"It's almost dark now," she said, looking up at me. "I think we should head back home."

"Oh... I was thinking we should run away."

Anna laughed and shook her head, and I rolled on my back, frowning in disappointment. We climbed off the hood and I stuffed the blanket back in the trunk before I slid into the driver's seat. Anna sighed, leaning her head back against the headrest while I pulled out of the turnaround and drove us back down the paved road. The radio played quietly while we sat in silence, and I wondered if Anna hated every second that brought us closer to her house like I did. But no matter how great the last month had been, or how amazing it was to go to prom and watch the sunset together—nothing could change these final moments from what they were: bitter, and mostly unfair.

When we reached Anna's house a short time later, I parked along the curb, though I was too deep in a mentally depressed spiral to look at her.

"Will you be back for Thanksgiving?" she asked.

"Yeah. We want to come back for the holidays."

"Okay... good. I'll be home from college, then."

"Cool. If you get busy and forget all about me... it's okay."

Anna made a mocking noise, and I finally glanced at her as she rolled her eyes.

"You're going to forget all about *me* when you're rich and famous and have tons of girls throwing themselves at you."

I smiled a little—hardly able to believe I could do such a thing in our final minute together.

"Maybe you could live in California one day?" I asked, trying not to sound too hopeful.

"Maybe. Will you come back to Florida if it doesn't work out there?"

"Possibly."

Anna sighed, and when she grabbed the door handle, I took her other hand closest to me.

"We're never going to forget each other," I said seriously. "I hate that we won't see each other for a while, but this isn't the end."

Anna shook her head quickly, her eyes slightly red and tearing up.

"No, it's not. Everything is turning out the way it's meant to. Goodnight, Adam."

SEVEN YEARS LATER

MAGIC | Adam

Eighty thousand fans threw their arms in the air and screamed as I finished the last note of my guitar riff, blinded by the bright lights surrounding the stage. The screeching note echoed through the speakers into the masses while I held my electric guitar over my head, walking with Nate toward Dex at the front of the stage. London's crowd was the largest of our sold out, nine-month world tour, but not a single fan seemed ready for the end of our two and a half hour show.

"We love our freaks!" Dex shouted in the mic. "You know it's Adam's *birthday* today—give him all your *filthy love!*"

Waves of screams hit us as hundreds of hands shot up from around the stage. The three of us immediately spread out, and while I touched as many hands as I could, I noticed a girl with choppy blonde hair and bright red lips fighting to get near me. I held my hand out to her when she made it through the crowd, but she wrapped her fingers tightly around my wrist and pulled.

"Kiss me!" she shouted. "I love you *so much!*"

Without a second thought, I dropped down on all fours, her arms sliding around my neck as our lips locked. Her mouth pressed hard against mine, and when she pulled back, her face glowed as she grinned.

"Happy birthday, Adam! You are so *amazing!*"

I jumped up and grabbed more hands, then gave the rock n' roll salute with Nate and Dex in the final minutes of our tour, which had had more than a hundred shows. We turned and jogged toward the giant black curtains behind us, passing through them into darkness before Nate opened a door into a bright hallway. The roar of our fans was a low rumble through the concrete walls while we walked down the hall to a large break room on the right side.

When we stepped in, I saw crew assistants and other stadium workers standing around a long buffet table as they ate and talked, and our manager—Tom Shultz—rapidly paced back and forth as he talked on his phone in front of a tall glass wall that overlooked the front of the stadium.

"I can't believe it's all over," Dex said behind me. "Most of it is a blur, but some moments are glued inside my brain forever."

"Yeah—kind of like the kiss I had with that hot girl right after the show," I bragged, turning around. "You guys saw that, right? She was shoving people to get to me."

"She wasn't hot. Just a five, man," Nate replied.

"What? No—a seven, at least," I countered.

"Too bad I missed your true love kiss," Dex said. "But a seven is only close to being hot. I bet she was mediocre."

Nate laughed, and I shot him a dirty look while Dex smirked.

We all wore ripped jeans that night, and Dex's green shirt had an ape-like monster head on it, which he wore beneath an unbuttoned black waistcoat. Nate's white t-shirt had the Rebel Riot band logo, and an orange bandana was tied around his forehead. My shirt was black with red sleeves that reached down to the middle of my forearm, and I wore a studded belt like I had in high school.

"We're still going to Vanessa's party tonight, right?" Dex asked.

"Sure," I said gruffly. "Where's it at?"

"Top floor of the 570 Club—it's a super hot place in London right now. We can go around ten when it starts."

"What happens when we're back in the US?" Nate teased. "How will you go without your favorite European score?"

I blinked before my gaze narrowed on Dex.

"You slept with Vanessa? When—"

"We got our own hotel room after you passed out last night. It was paradise, man."

I furrowed my eyebrows, unable to remember much about our small party—mainly because of all the pills and alcohol I swallowed. But before I could ask more, Shultz walked up to us, his expression annoyed. He had a handsome face and a gray streak through his black hair, and his designer suits always clashed with anything we wore.

"We need to leave in ten minutes," he said firmly, his eyes flashing between us. "The magazine writer can't possibly wait a second past nine o'clock. Security is ready, so grab your things."

"How many leeches are outside?" Nate asked.

"Don't worry about them. They won't interfere."

Almost a hundred journalists and paparazzi had been waiting at the stadium when we arrived earlier that day, and now that several hours had passed, there were probably a lot more.

The three of us split up and I walked toward the buffet table, grabbing a water bottle and stepping into the private bathroom a few feet away. The inside was small and square-shaped, and after locking the door, I ignored my reflection and sunk down on the toilet lid. It felt good to be alone for a few minutes, but I hardly relaxed while I dug into my pocket for the pill baggy. When I saw the five powdery blue ovals inside it, my heart pounded excitedly.

Finally—I wish I could slip some blue magic on stage.

I opened the water bottle and washed down three pills, then pressed my forehead against my palms as I leaned forward. Nate and Dex never struggled with our packed schedule, or cared that Shultz controlled every bit of it—something that always ate at me. But I didn't want the money to stop pouring in anymore than they did—I just—

Quit being pathetic. I'm twenty-five now—I can handle this. It's all for the fans, anyway. They freakin' love us, and

I'm not letting anyone down. So what if Shultz runs my life? We wouldn't be where we are without everything he's done...

Intense heat spread over my body as my anxiety climbed, mixing with the hate I had for being controlled every day for the last six years. I glared at the bathroom door—wishing I could rip it off the hinges and break it to pieces—but I grabbed the pill baggy instead, wondering if I just needed more blue magic.

Why isn't it working yet?

I stuffed the baggy in my pocket and stood up, deciding to finally look at myself in the mirror above the sink. Thankfully, I didn't look as terrible as I felt, but the purplish-blue wedges under my eyes had gotten larger, and my cheeks were still hollow. I frowned and stared at the sink drain, hardly able to remember when I could look at my face for more than a few seconds. No one ever said anything about how I looked—even though Shultz, Nate, and Dex knew why—and I doubted it mattered, so long as I was able to perform concerts and handle interviews.

The only way out is to quit, but I'm never doing that. I just need to bury the rage and deal with it. I can enjoy our success when I'm old—not now. I have to keep going, or wait until Nate and Dex have had enough...

And then I felt it—the tingling in my hands that always started when the blue magic hit my system. I grinned as I waited for it to reach my brain, and completely change my energy and mood. But before it happened, a knock on the door surprised me.

"Adam? You in there?" I heard Dex ask. "Come on, man—Shultz is going to lose it."

* * * * * *

The clock on the SUV dash read 10:04 pm as our chauffeur drove us through the glowing city of London after our magazine interview. I sat in the back seat between Nate and Dex while we laughed manically and passed a fifth of vodka back and forth.

"What does the precious birthday boy want most this year?" Dex teased, tousling my hair. "Maybe Vanessa has a toy train nicely wrapped up for you."

Nate snickered as I brought the fifth to my lips, rolling my eyes.

"Damn it—I don't want a *train*," I said, disappointed. "Can your girlfriend be my toy, instead?"

An animal-like cry escaped Dex's throat as he put his hands around my neck and pretended to strangle me. Nate roared with laughter while I tried to push Dex away, and when he stopped trying to kill me a minute later, Nate poked me in the ribs.

"Got any blue magic?" he asked.

I nodded and pulled the baggy out of my pocket, placing it in his lap with the fifth of vodka. Nate chased the last two pills with a long swig and slipped the almost empty bottle in the pocket of the passenger seat in front of him. I then noticed the SUV was slowing down, and within minutes, we were parked in front of a brick building lit up by pink and purple neon lights.

Nate's door faced the entrance to the club, and after he climbed out onto the street, I stood up—surprised that the SUV felt like it was rocking. Dex pushed me and I stumbled toward the open door, taking a careless step out. Within seconds, I was lying on my side on top of the cement, my right shoulder throbbing.

"What the h-hell?" I said, laughing. "Why is the s-sidewalk so hard?"

"You're not supposed to get cozy with it, moron," Nate replied. "Get up!"

I rolled onto all fours and struggled to lift myself back onto my feet, then followed Nate and Dex toward the club doors. A long line of people waited along the left side of the building, and one of the three bouncers who guarded the door immediately waved us in. The crowd cheered as we passed them and walked through the golden doors, entering into a small, circular room lit by rectangular light panels on the walls. A woman with short, straight hair and a shiny black dress stood next to another door with a tablet in hand, her smile pleasant and knowing.

"Welcome to the 570 Club," she said in a silky voice. "Adam, Dex, Nate—follow me to your party, please."

We walked wordlessly behind her into the next room, which was square and white and had strange black sculptures in each corner. Music vibrated from two solid black doors in front of us, and as I wondered what kind of party jammed on the other side, our hostess turned left toward an elevator. The silver doors slid apart after she scanned an ID card, and we all stepped inside the large box.

While the elevator traveled up, the silence between me, Nate, and Dex felt deafening compared to the SUV earlier, but I could sense none of us were sure what to do in front of the pretty hostess. The ride to the top floor was quick, and when the doors rolled open, we faced a dimly lit purple hallway filled with doors.

"Vanessa's party is through the red door at the end of the hall," the woman informed. "Would you like anything sent up for you?"

"Um—yeah—your number," Nate blurted.

The hostess grinned as me and Dex burst out laughing, and after she tapped at her tablet, Nate's cell phone dinged.

"Wish granted," she replied happily. "That's the number to the front desk. If I'm there, I'll answer your call."

Nate groaned as me and Dex grabbed his arms and led him out of the elevator. When we were alone in the hall, Dex slapped his back.

"At least she was straight with you, man," he said.

"Whatever," Nate replied. "I *will* call the front desk—just wait."

We reached the red door at the end of the hall, and I twisted the golden knob, stepping into the party with Nate and Dex behind me. The large room was mostly black and had almost a hundred people inside, standing around the bar in the back or sitting on chairs and couches. Different colored spotlights created circles of light on the carpet, and a private DJ played techno music next to the bar.

"Dex! You naughty boy."

Vanessa walked out of the crowd toward us, her soft voice with an English accent sounding playfully annoyed. She wore a pink party dress that clung to her tall, skinny body, and her blonde hair was wrapped in a tight bun on top of her head. The large silver hoops that hung from her ears also framed her porcelain, doll-like face.

"What'd I do?" Dex asked, wrapping an arm around her.

"You didn't tell me it was Adam's birthday," she said, crossing her arms. "Now I don't have a gift for him."

"Don't worry, Vanessa," I replied. "Just give me a kiss."

The model raised her eyebrows, then shot Dex a look.

"You should be punished," she told him with a smile. "I have to do as he asks, now."

Dex sighed and frowned.

"Just make it quick," he grumbled. "And maybe I won't kill him."

Vanessa laughed and skipped in front of me, her lips pressing firmly into mine. I fought an urge to pull her against me, but her kiss quickly ended.

"You know... maybe there is something I can do for you, and a friend," she said coolly. "Want some privacy with a fan tonight?"

I raised a brow, the corner of my mouth turning upward.

"Depends. She as pretty as you?"

Vanessa made a desperate sound and flicked her eyes toward the ceiling.

"She's *gorgeous*. I'll be right back."

The beautiful blonde turned and left us, and I suddenly stumbled sideways from a punch in the arm.

"What the hell, man?" Nate barked at me. "You get a free kiss from Vanessa and now she's hooking you up? This is bull!"

I laughed and rubbed my arm, seeing double as my gaze flashed between him and Dex.

"Fly to the UK on your birthday," I replied. "Or have Vanessa talk the hostess into—"

I stopped talking when Vanessa appeared in front of us again, holding the hand of another model who looked strangely familiar. The new girl had straight brown hair and soft facial features, her gray eyes haunting me. Her black dress was strapless and short, and the fabric around her waist was see-through. My good time melted into paranoia as I stared at her, convinced that I was seeing a ghost from years ago.

"Adam, this is..."

Vanessa's voice was lost in my racing thoughts, though I heard something about one of the hallway suites. I finally managed to focus a minute later, when her friend stepped toward me, smiling.

"It's amazing to meet you," she said excitedly. "Ready to go... relax?"

I nodded and ran a hand through my hair, forcing myself back into some kind of sanity.

"Yeah—let's go."

The brunette model followed behind me into the purple hall, and I turned the knobs of the suites near us, trying not to look at her.

"Your last show was today, wasn't it?" she asked.

"Uh, yeah—the tour is over finally."

"How does it feel? Wasn't it almost a year long?"

I nodded and tried a third door knob, but it was locked. I sighed heavily and turned around, frustrated.

"I can't find a damn room. What's your name?"

She stared at me in surprise, her face and figure still a perfect reminder of someone else.

"It's Anna," she said.

My eyes widened as my anxiety surged, causing the hair on the back of my neck to stand up.

"What? Your name is *Anna?*"

"No—I'm *Ava.*"

"But you said Anna."

"No, I didn't. You misheard me."

"Prove it."

Anna—or *Ava*—immediately frowned, her eyebrows furrowing.

"Why? Are you okay?"

"You just—you look like someone I know."

"Oh..."

"Forget it. Is that door open?"

Ava turned to her right and twisted the knob I pointed at, causing a sudden *click* to fill the air. She smiled at me and walked inside, but I took a deep breath before following her.

Quit freaking out. I guess I shouldn't hook up after pills and alcohol...

I closed the door behind me and stared at the suite, which was a large pink room with a bed, private bar, and mirrored ceiling. The stocked bar was built into the wall on the left side of the room, and a silver stripping pole stood in the open area several feet in front of the bed. While I walked toward the end of the bed and sat down, Ava went to the bar and started making drinks. My left leg bounced anxiously as I waited for her, and less than a minute later, she slid down beside me, placing a short glass in my hand.

"Do you like whiskey sours?" she asked curiously.

I nodded and we sipped our glasses together, but even though I liked the drink she'd made, I hardly wanted it.

"You ready?" I asked.

Ava smiled and wiped her upper lip, then set her glass on the floor. She closed her eyes as I leaned into her, my hand pulling at the zipper on the back of her dress.

SECRETS | Anna

I watched the glowing city of Los Angeles through a large window in my studio while I took a break from working on my latest dress, the Sapphire Nova. It hung nearly finished on a torso mannequin a few feet away, and was made of glossy navy fabric with an elegant lace back and flowing train. The top layer of the skirt was decorated with silver stitching in the shape of thick, elongated swirls, and I had outlined them with small, rounded pieces of glass that reflected light like distant stars in the galaxy.

The Sapphire Nova was my best creation for Solva's upcoming fall collection of ball gowns and evening dress, and I hoped it would be officially chosen by Keller Aston, the director of my team of concept designers.

I turned from the window when the studio door opened, smiling at my coworker Bristol as she carried two mugs of hot tea toward me. Her naturally red hair was long and wound into a messy bun, and she wore an oversized knitted sweater and jeans. My hair was swept back into a ponytail, and I wore a black fleece jacket over my plain t-shirt, as well as jeans and flats. Bristol handed me one of the mugs and returned to her spot on the couch across the room, placing her sketchbook back on her lap.

"When the right idea hits, my dress will come together like a whirlwind," she said confidently. "I can't believe you're almost done with yours."

I smiled, shrugging.

"I got lucky this time—I felt like I knew exactly what I needed to do."

"Yeah, I hope that happens to me, too. I don't care if I have to spend every day and night here for the next week."

I grinned and sipped at my tea, turning back toward the window as Bristol began to sketch. But I wasn't lost in my thoughts for long before I heard her gasp.

"I can't believe Maggie," she said, annoyed. "When is she going to realize Steven doesn't want anything serious? I'm tired of her complaining about it."

"Oh—is she texting you?"

"Yeah. He only wants to hook up with her, and she gives in *every* time, then whines about not being his girlfriend."

Bristol rolled her eyes and started typing on her cell screen as I turned away again. Although I had been friends with her for almost three months, she didn't know that I was still a virgin, and that I'd made the decision to wait for marriage at the age of twenty. It was something I purposely told no one outside of my church group, though mostly as a protective measure since very few still understood that particular desire. And fortunately, the subject hadn't come up much between us, as it was easy to talk to Bristol about almost anything else during the course of the work day.

"Do you keep a guy on the side?" she asked.

My heart started pounding as I stared out the window, but I forced my expression to stay calm as it seemed the moment had finally come.

"No... do you?"

I glanced at Bristol, who shook her head.

"Not at the moment. I broke up with the last guy I dated before I started working here."

"What happened?"

"He just became a jerk, like they all do."

She frowned and started sketching, and I left the large window, having too much on my mind suddenly to stay late any longer. I grabbed my purse from the bottom drawer of my desk and slipped the strap over my shoulder.

"Thanks for the tea," I said. "I'm ready to go home, but I'm taking it with me."

"Aw—don't leave," she teased. "Are we the only ones here?"

"I think so, besides security."

"Okay. I'll try to get a rough sketch done and then I'm going home."

"Sounds good. I'll see you tomorrow."

I walked toward the studio door and stepped into the hall, making my way past empty offices and conference rooms to the elevator at the end. The studio of my design team was on the fourth floor of Solva headquarters, and staying late to work on potential collection pieces was the norm for all of us. When I finally stood alone inside the elevator, I took a deep breath and rubbed my eyes, torn between my secret and the way of the world.

It wasn't always like this... a lot more people used to save their intimacy for marriage less than a hundred years ago. Why did that change? Why does no one care about waiting for that special person they'll be with forever?

I stared at my feet, trying to pretend like I didn't know the answer—or that I experienced my own feelings of doubt about what I wanted.

Because it's hard—really hard sometimes, and it doesn't help that sex is everywhere. I mean, I couldn't even watch that medieval show last night because naked women were everywhere in it. But I guess if I didn't grow up in church, I never would have learned about pure intimacy, and made my choice before it was too late...

The doors to the elevator slid open, and I walked into the empty lobby of the first floor, waving at the security officers behind their desk before I left the building. The large parking lot to the right of Solva headquarters was practically empty as I quickly walked across it and climbed inside my green Cherokee. I locked the doors and sat in silence, captivated by a certain thought that always intrigued and terrified me when I thought about my secret dream.

What would Adam think?

● ● ● ● ● ●

Two weeks later, Bristol and I sat in the conference room at Solva with the other concept artists as our director, Keller Aston, handed back everyone's sketch books with notes. He was a tall man with bleached hair, red glasses, and a nice suit, and I noticed he seemed more excitable than usual that morning.

"Because of the fine work being produced by this team, three dresses have already been chosen for the fall collection next November," he said happily, returning to his place at the head of the table. "Two others are in special consideration, but if your dress was chosen—you will find out today."

The ten of us stopped flipping through our sketch books and stared at him.

"If you find a pink sticky note somewhere on your desk, then your dress is in the fall collection! If you find a blue one, your piece is in special consideration."

We continued to stare at him in tense silence, and Keller sighed dramatically.

"Go on—search your desks! I have nothing further to say, except that I am extremely proud of all of you."

I immediately rose to my feet and followed everyone out of the conference room, heading down the hall toward the design studios. The one Bristol and I worked in was at the end of the hall, and once we made it inside, we started searching our desks for a sticky note.

"I don't see one!" I heard Bristol exclaim. "How well do you think he hid them?"

"I don't know," I said frantically, opening all my drawers. "Maybe our dresses weren't good enough?"

"I worked really hard to finish mine last week, but I guess that's not—*I found a pink sticky note!*"

My heart pounded as I stared across the room at Bristol, who danced beside her desk and held it in the air. Her dress—which she'd managed to pull together in the last two weeks—was ice blue with a shimmering tulle skirt and lace bodice that had leaves and icicles embroidered into it.

"Where did you find that?" I asked frantically.

"It was *under* my desk!"

I blinked and dropped to my hands and knees, searching the carpet beneath my desk for a pink piece of paper—but finding nothing. I sighed heavily and sat on the floor—fully heartbroken in an instant—until I saw a pink sticky note hanging from under the top surface of my desk. With a gasp, I grabbed it and jumped up.

"The Sapphire Nova was picked!" I shouted. "We're both going to be in the collection!"

Bristol squealed and skipped over to me, our arms wrapping around each other as we jumped up and down.

"We're getting drinks tonight to celebrate!" she said. "I'll invite Maggie, too, so you can meet her."

I nodded, forcing myself to keep smiling.

"Great! Where should we go?"

"We like The Frisk House," she said. "Have you been there?"

"No. Why is it called that?"

Bristol laughed. "They serve special fries called frisky fries. Don't worry—no one will actually frisk you."

I sighed with exaggerated relief, and for the rest of the work day, we gushed about our dresses being chosen as we made the fine-tuned adjustments according to Keller's notes in our sketchbooks.

● ● ● ● ● ●

When I arrived at the Frisk House a little after seven that night, Bristol and Maggie were already waiting inside. The small but lively restaurant was brightly lit through many of its large glass windows, and the exterior was a combination of dark wood and metal slabs. The restaurant name glowed white in cursive letters against a black metal background, and when I opened one of the glass double doors, I walked toward the host standing behind the front desk.

"Hi," I said loudly above the music. "I'm part of Bristol Doyle's party."

"Excellent. Welcome to the Frisk House," the young man said, dressed in a black button-up shirt and trousers. "Right this way."

I trailed behind him as he led me through the crowded restaurant, which had a lot of booths, high tops, and large flat screens mounted to the walls. Bristol's table was at the far end of the open room, and when she and Maggie saw me, they waved excitedly.

"Hey!" Bristol said as I slid down into their booth. "Anna—this is Maggie."

I smiled at the young woman sitting next to her, though her shocking appearance forced me to hide my surprise. Despite being blonde, thin, and having a large cup size, Maggie's pale eyebrows were colored heavily with brown pencil, and her lips looked uncomfortably enlarged from filler injections. Her professionally whitened teeth were jagged and overlapped, and her tan—which was several shades too dark—made me think she had an obsession with tanning beds. It was almost hard to look at her and Bristol side by side, for Maggie's unnatural look contrasted sharply with Bristol's pale skin and delicate feminine features.

"It's so nice to meet you," Maggie said in awe. "You and Bristol are *amazing* for getting your dresses into the fall collection next year. I can't even draw a stick figure!"

Bristol laughed. "It doesn't matter how well you can draw in fashion—you have to be good at sewing."

"I can't even do that," Maggie assured. "But you better get me a ticket for the fashion show, because I'll die if I miss it!"

I smiled at her enthusiasm, shifting my gaze to the waitress suddenly at our table. Once Bristol and Maggie ordered, I stopped scanning the menu.

"I'll have buffalo wings and two vodka shots with cranberry juice," I said quickly.

After the waitress jotted down my order and left, I noticed Maggie staring at her phone with a worried expression.

"Steven wants me to come over after this," she said. "He says he wants to *talk*."

Bristol immediately rolled her eyes.

"Don't do it," she said, annoyed. "You know he's only saying that to get you over there for the night. Tell him he finally has to commit or you'll never see him again."

Maggie nodded, but still looked anxious.

"Why don't my feelings mean anything to him?" she pressed. "He knows I love him and would do anything for him, but that's not enough to be exclusive? Maybe I just need to be more patient and see what he has to say tonight."

I gave her a sympathetic look and waited for Bristol to respond, but Maggie stared at me in the silence.

"Should I go?" she asked me. "What if Steven wants to commit and I bail out?"

"What does he want to talk about?" I asked.

"I don't know—he won't tell me. He just wants me to come over."

"Yeah, because he doesn't want to talk about being exclusive," Bristol insisted. "Tell him what I said and don't let him use you."

Maggie looked at her phone and started typing, then hesitated.

"I just need to go," she urged. "I haven't seen him in over a week and if he wants to talk, that's fine. I *won't* stay the night, though."

"Good luck," Bristol replied.

As Maggie texted Steven back, I wondered if I should tell them *my* approach to relationships... and how ridiculous they might find it. But I didn't like hiding my dream, and if I could help them in some way, I knew it would be worth it.

"A long time ago... I decided to save myself for marriage," I confessed, slowly. "So, I'm not an expert on guys like Steven, but I'm looking for someone who has been waiting too, or at least... will be patient enough to wait for me."

Bristol raised her eyebrows in mild surprise before her expression became neutral, and Maggie's jaw dropped slightly.

"That's interesting," she said. "Why did you—"

"Because you're a Christian, right?" Bristol asked, interrupting.

I nodded. "Yeah, and I know waiting for marriage isn't that popular anymore... but it's the choice I've made."

Both of them were silent for a few long seconds, and eventually, Bristol nodded.

"I used to think I'd wait for marriage, too," she replied, this time surprising me. "I grew up in church, but things changed, you know?"

I nodded politely, and for the next few hours, the three of us enjoyed our drinks and ate. It had felt good to share my secret without criticism, but I knew neither of them had been convinced. Before we left that night, I saw a concert clip of Rebel Riot play on one of the flat screens—a reminder of yet another unmentioned truth.

Along with my desire to save sex for marriage, which I admitted sparingly, I'd never bothered to tell anyone that I knew Adam Avery, or that we'd crushed on each other in high school. It seemed even more pointless and difficult to discuss than my other shocking truth—especially since he and his band mates were little more than ghosts to me now. But I had always been glad that they achieved their impossible dream years ago, and I wished Adam had some way of knowing I had pursued mine.

ADDICT | Adam

I stared at the sky through dark sunglasses, bare-chested and wearing cutoff shorts as I laid on a reclining chair next to my pool. It felt good to be alone for a while since returning to the United States two weeks ago, but even after an international flight and fourteen days, I was still thinking about Anna—whose ghost had suddenly started to haunt me.

What does she think of me now? I guess that depends on who she is... and if she believes the tabloids, which never have all the facts.

I closed my eyes and let my body go limp under the sun, remembering Anna as a freshman in college years ago, when I'd last spoken to her. And after all this time, I didn't have any reason to think she'd changed her mind about accounting... but I felt a crazy, hungry urge to *believe* she had.

Damn it, Anna—you loved fashion and had talent for it. You better not be crunching numbers somewhere, like you're ordinary...

I grabbed my cell off the table next to me and stared at the screen, hoping to see a text from Hazel that I knew she hadn't sent yet. Despite her promise to stop by with more pills earlier, it was almost six and I still hadn't heard anything. I dropped my phone on the table and groaned, endlessly tortured by my merciless need.

What the hell is she doing? I can't wait another day for more magic. Three days without is too long...

My half empty beer sat on the pavement next to my chair, and while I finished off the can, my cell suddenly dinged. I swiped it from the table and sat up instantly, knocking off my sunglasses as I read the new text message.

MOM: what wine do you want for dinner?

● ● ● ● ● ●

I parked my black Range Rover in front of my mom's house in Beverly Hills around seven thirty that night. She lived only twenty minutes away on Carmelita Avenue with her rich investor husband, Rob Saxton, who she'd married four years ago. Their large Spanish style house had curved orange shingles, white stucco siding, and decorative outdoor tiles, along with a private gate that I opened with a remote.

After walking to the front door, I let myself into the wide, minimally decorated foyer. A large picture frame with a collage of photos sat propped on a table against the left wall, and while I took a second to see who was in it, I heard the clack of heels leaving the kitchen at the end of the foyer.

"Adam! Honey, how are you? I've missed you a lot."

My mother walked toward me in a casual red dress and black high heels, her blonde and brown streaked hair pulled back by a large clip. When she hugged me, I wrapped my arms around her tightly.

"I'm fine," I said plainly. "The tour was amazing, but it almost killed me."

"I watched a few of your concerts," she said excitedly. "Did you know they were offered as paid TV specials?"

"No—what'd you think?"

"You can really stir up a crowd!" she replied with a laugh. "But it's always great to see you boys doing what you love. I decided to make shrimp Alfredo tonight—I thought it would be a nice surprise."

I grinned.

"Definitely. It smells great in here."

My mom smiled and pinched my chin with her thumb and index finger, shaking my head slightly like she did when I was ten.

"When Rob gets home, I'll have him hang that picture frame on the wall," she said, gesturing toward the collage. "Did you see your prom picture in there?"

I shook my head, trying to fight back the anxiety of Anna's ghost again.

"I went through a box of photos last week and decided to put the best ones together like this. I thought this picture of you and Andrea was precious."

"Her name isn't Andrea... it's... Anna."

My mother blinked, then nodded.

"That's right—Anna! I thought she was very sweet."

I looked at the collage again and stared at the prom picture, which showed us smiling and standing close together in front of a small lake.

"It's kind of strange... but I've been thinking about her for the last few weeks," I admitted.

"Oh? What is she doing these days?"

I shrugged. "Don't know exactly, but she went to college for accounting."

"I suppose she's doing that, then. Let's go to the kitchen."

We left the foyer and walked into the kitchen a short distance away, which was a large room with white cabinets, marble countertops, and stainless steel appliances.

"The noodles still need a few minutes," my mother said as she stepped in front of the stove. "But everything will be ready in the next half hour."

I nodded and slid down onto a stool, watching the news on a mounted flat screen across the room as I ate from a bowl of almonds.

"I don't want you to get upset, Adam," my mother said suddenly. "But... I've been worried about a few things I've seen."

I furrowed my eyebrows, confused.

"Like what?"

She sighed heavily. "I know the tabloids exaggerate a lot, but there have been articles claiming that you—*and* Nate and Dex—did all kinds of drugs on the tour. Is that true?"

I rolled my eyes and grunted.

"No, of course not. We obviously partied and had fun, but we weren't snorting coke or doing heroin. Those stupid magazines say anything to make money."

My mother nodded quickly, but she didn't look convinced.

"I've never done hard drugs," I added, annoyed. "I know what kind of damage they do and I'm not stupid."

"I know you're not," she said, pouring the pot of noodles into a strainer in the sink. "But you still need to be very careful about what you're exposed to. Sex, drugs, and rock n' roll isn't just a saying—it's a dangerous lifestyle."

"Yeah, I know. Don't worry. I'm not doing anything that will ruin my life."

"You better not. Rob should be here any minute."

While my mom carried the strainer from the sink to the stove, my whole body tensed as I felt my cell vibrate in my pocket. I pulled it out carefully and glanced at the screen—a text from Hazel making my heart pound.

HAZEL: At ur house. Where are u?

ME: i'm close by. give me a sec and i'll be right there.

"Can you set the table?" my mom asked.

I stood up and shook my head, desperate for a good excuse to leave.

"I need to go home real quick—a plumber just showed up to fix a leak."

"What leak? It's eight o'clock at night."

"I'll be right back, okay?"

I started to leave the kitchen, but my mother's voice stopped me.

"Do you really need to go? Dinner is done now."

A muscle in my jaw tightened as I tried not glare at her.

"Yeah—*I do.* Rob isn't here yet, anyway."

I left the kitchen and rushed through the foyer, then out the front door. I felt relieved as I walked toward my Range Rover—happy to finally escape—but bright headlights suddenly turned into the driveway. Rob parked his red BMW beside my car, and I gritted my teeth as he shut off the engine and climbed out.

"Adam!" he said energetically. "How are you, killer?"

He was in his mid-fifties and had short brown hair and a nicely combed beard, and he wore his usual pinstriped suit as he walked over to me.

"Fine—I just need to run home real quick."

"How was the tour? Wild, right?"

"Insane," I said quickly, opening my car door. "I'll tell you about it when I get back."

"Why? Off to meet your drug dealer?"

My body immediately went rigid as I sat in the driver's seat of the Range Rover, feeling short of breath while Rob's words twisted my gut.

"What's that look for?" he said with a laugh. "I'm kidding! But you're almost old enough for The 27 Club. Don't join them, okay?"

He turned and walked toward the house, and I closed the car door, starting the Range Rover with my hand shaking.

Get a grip—he doesn't actually know what I'm doing. Blue magic isn't a big deal, but he and my mom would still freak if they knew. Everyone has something that makes them happy, and this is no different...

When I turned onto the road, I drove ten miles over the speed limit, but the twenty minute drive home still felt twice as long. It didn't help that I was paranoid about getting a text from Hazel, telling me she'd gotten tired of waiting and left. I couldn't imagine another day without the pills, and I knew if I couldn't get them from her that night, I would have to spend all of tomorrow hunting her down. But I finally relaxed when I turned into my driveway a short time later, seeing her silver Yukon parked in front of the garage.

I'd left the front door unlocked for her, and after climbing out of the Range Rover, I quickly made my way inside the house. The glass foyer led directly into the living room where I saw Hazel lying on the couch, her feet propped up on the armrest in black boots.

"Adam!" she said happily, sitting up. "How's my favorite rock star?"

"I'm good," I said casually. "I hope you haven't waited long."

She shook her head, her straight black hair hardly moving. Hazel had a short, tanned, and bony body, and she wore a gray tank top with a large Chanel emblem, along with a black denim skirt and knee-high laced boots.

"I haven't," she stated. "But your place is one of my nicest stops, so I don't care. If you took much longer, I was going to check out your home theater."

"You can hang out in there any time," I said. "How many pills do you have?"

She stood from the couch and walked toward me, stopping with only inches of space between us.

"I got enough. Do you want the usual amount?"

"No—I'll take twenty more."

"That'll cost six hundred, then. Do you have that?"

"Of course."

I reached in my pocket and took out a folded wad of ten one hundred dollar bills, handing six of them to Hazel. She walked back to the couch and opened her purse, where she stayed for a few minutes until she brought me a new baggy of blue magic. My heart pounded in excitement as I took it from her, my eyes locked on the small blue ovals that could do what nothing else ever had.

"How many of these are too much?" I asked curiously.

"Too much? You mean, for an overdose?"

"Yeah. I've taken three before without a problem, but what about four, or five?"

Hazel shrugged.

"I'm not a doctor, Adam. But if you can handle three, then probably a few more won't hurt."

I nodded and stared at the pills, wondering if I should swallow a few now or wait until Hazel left. But she stood in front of me in silence, and eventually, I looked at her.

"It used to be cool to tell my friends that I knew you," she said, her tone unusually soft. "But now, I think it would be better to say—"

"What? You want to spend the night?"

A guilty smile spread across her face, but she shook her head.

"No. I don't sleep with buyers because they think they don't have to pay me, which is *never* true. But... if I kissed you, it would still drive my friends mad."

"Sure. Make them suffer."

Hazel squealed and stood on her toes, pressing her lips hard into mine like a statue. She kissed me longer than I expected, and when she finally pulled back, she wiped her lip gloss from my mouth with her finger.

"A pleasure doing any and all things with you," she teased, going back to the couch to grab her purse. "Bye now, Adam."

I waved quickly as she walked around me and out the front door, then I headed straight for the kitchen. I grabbed a glass out of the cabinet and filled it with water, excited to try four pills instead of three—especially since I'd been without them for seventy-two hours. But the high I expected would be too much to drive, and although I felt terrible about it, I quickly sent a text to my mom, telling her I couldn't make it back for dinner.

SHOCK | Anna

My high school days with Adam played and rewound inside my mind like a vintage home video, choppily edited and stored away years ago—but never lost.

The day after drinks with Bristol and Maggie at the Frisk House, I returned to my apartment around five-thirty after work and went straight to my bedroom. While I rummaged through my dresser and changed into a t-shirt and pajama shorts, it seemed like almost every memory of Adam and I replayed before my eyes, eventually reminding me of our separation after graduation—and how I thought I loved him during my first semester at college that fall.

Who wouldn't think they were in love with their first serious crush? I thought he was so cool and intriguing back then... but now, we're too many worlds apart. What we used to have wouldn't be possible now. Everything that's said about him is awful, and I failed at being a light to him...

With a heavy frown, I left my bedroom and walked into the kitchen, where I grabbed a plastic bag of popcorn kernels from the cupboard. Bristol would be coming over soon to watch a movie, and I planned to ask why she had changed her mind about premarital sex—even though the idea made butterflies whirl inside my stomach.

How long did she try to save herself? I hate that it changed for her—I can't imagine ever giving up, but maybe she'll understand me a lot more than others have.

I took a tall pot out of the cupboard next to the stove and poured oil and a few cups of kernels inside it, placing the lid on top and turning on the burner. But instead of leaving until the kernels popped, I stared through the glass lid, my mind still heavy in thought.

How many women has Adam been with? Not a lot, I hope, but he is a famous rock star... so tons, probably. Is that really him, though? Is he anything like high school, or is he completely different? I wish we could talk again, even if it was just once. He's still a friend, and someone special...

I left the kitchen and walked into my bedroom, where I pulled my cell phone out of my purse. I quickly opened my internet browser and typed in "Adam Avery"—then scrolled through hundreds of pictures while my pulse raced. Although I normally tried to avoid any news or research about him, there had been a few times I'd given into the urge, and tonight was the first in more than a year.

I smiled as I scrolled through mostly concert and event photos of him, usually with Nate and Dex at his side. His body had thickened since high school, and his long, dyed locks were still side-swept like I remembered, with a few pieces hanging in front of his face. But despite my strong, unwavering attraction to him, I couldn't ignore the dark marks I'd noticed beneath his eyes a while ago, along with the unnatural hollowness of his cheeks.

While I studied more pictures of him, I thought his eyes looked dull as he smiled, and that a hint of anger would come through his relaxed expressions as a slight frown.

The tabloids say he's doing drugs, and honestly... I believe it. He doesn't look very happy, or healthy. Come on, Adam—what are you thinking?

I sighed and turned off my cell screen, leaving my room as I followed the sound of kernels popping in the kitchen. There, I took a large bowl from the cupboard and melted half a stick of butter, which I poured over the popcorn after dumping it into the bowl.

I'm sure I'm nothing to him now. He's had a few girlfriends, and would probably laugh at my dream, which I don't think I could take. I wish we didn't have to lose each other, but even if I hadn't dated Will, I'm not sure we would have stayed close until now...

I took the large popcorn bowl into the living room and set it on the coffee table, then turned on the TV to see what free movies were available. But as I started going through them, a knock on my door made me stand up, and I smiled when I saw Bristol waiting on the other side of it.

"Hey!" I said, hugging her. "Welcome! I just made popcorn, so it's still hot."

She smiled and stepped inside, her gaze shifting around my white living room and kitchen, which were clean and minimally decorated.

"It's so cute in here," she gushed. "I love that you keep it simple. Sophie and I have crap everywhere."

"I usually have clothes and random things lying around," I confessed. "But I've been able to keep it clean for a few days."

We left the door and walked to the couch, where Bristol settled in the left corner and I sat in the middle, crossing my legs as I picked up the remote.

"What do you want to watch?" I asked.

"You can pick. I just want to relax for a while without listening to Sophie and Tyler argue."

"Oh—is he at your apartment?"

"No, but she keeps calling him every five minutes to fight about something and I'm over it."

"Yeah, that sounds annoying."

I grabbed the large popcorn bowl from the coffee table and set it between us, then chose a space movie I'd recently seen and loved. We watched the first half hour in silence—except for the crunching of popcorn—and I steadily worked up the courage to ask her the question that had bothered me.

"Bristol—you said at the bar that you once tried to save yourself for marriage?"

My cheeks felt hot once the words left my mouth, and I glanced at her, but she seemed undisturbed.

"I did," she replied. "But that's a really hard standard to live up to—especially when you think you're in love."

"Yeah… I'm sure," I said slowly. "So, you changed your mind because you loved someone?"

"Well, I thought I did, but that was a huge mistake."

"Oh. Do you wish you hadn't slept with him, then?"

She shrugged, her eyes on the TV as she ate a few bites of popcorn.

"No—I've had sex with other guys since, and the worst part has always been when it doesn't work out. Sometimes sex makes the breakup harder, but I don't wish I was a virgin again."

I nodded and stared blankly at the movie as I tried to make sense of her perspective.

"I can't believe how far you've made it, Anna," she added. "I guess you've never been in love?"

I blinked and raised my eyebrows, quickly hiding my unexpected offense.

"Not truly, no," I admitted. "But saving myself for marriage is something I really want to do, so... I hope I can no matter what."

"Okay. I'm just not sure a lot of guys will understand. Hardly anyone lives like that anymore."

"I know," I said, trying to keep my calm. "But I'm only going to find the right person if I stay true to myself, right?"

"Yeah, I guess," she replied. "You'll probably have to marry someone at church, then. I hope you don't end up with someone boring and sheltered."

Her words—possibly not meant to hurt me—sank like a knife into my gut, and inside, I exploded.

Boring and sheltered? You think men who value purity are worse than the animals you choose? You've missed the whole point! Excuse me for saving my intimacy for more than my latest fling, which I'd hate to see go up in flames like all of yours, Bristol!

"The men at my church are great," I replied happily with a tight smile. "I'd be lucky to marry one of them. We'll see what happens."

* * * * * *

While I stood alone in the elevator at Solva headquarters the next afternoon, the force of Bristol's words still cut into me, shredding most of the hope I had that she might understand my dream, even in some small way. But no matter how much the effort she'd given toward it, Bristol had ultimately changed her mind about premarital sex, and the heartache that followed wasn't enough to make her supportive of me.

I guess that's how it was meant to be for her—but it could have been so much better if she stuck it out. I mean, I don't know for sure, but I can't believe sleeping around is the better option. It seems only men win a lot in that scenario.

When the elevator doors opened, I stepped into the main lobby on the bottom floor and turned left, following a hallway that led to the cafeteria. I was eating lunch late that day, and few people were around as I made a chicken salad at the buffet, then walked outside into a nearby courtyard. It was square shaped with a variety of plants, and the ground had brick paths that led to four separate picnic tables.

I chose the nearest one and placed my cell next to me on the table, scrolling through one of my social media accounts as I ate my salad. Eventually, I noticed a small red dot above the message icon and tapped it.

`REBEL RIOT: hey, it's adam. been a long time.`

My eyes widened as my heart hammered through my chest, the air in my lungs nearly disappearing. I stared at the message as if I expected it to suddenly erase itself, and prove that I had somehow hallucinated. But after a few minutes, I blinked and shook my head, trying to come to grips with reality.

What's going on? This can't be Adam—not the real *Adam Avery. This is a joke, or spam, or something, but... what if it's real? It looks real, and it has been a long time since we talked...*

I took a deep breath and looked at the profile the message had come from, seeing that it was the official account of his band. I returned to the message and tapped the reply box, slowly typing out the first—and *only*—thing that had come to mind.

```
ME: Hi Adam! It's a surprise to hear from you.
We did it!
```

FOUND | Adam

After two weeks of being haunted by Anna's ghost and not knowing what happened to her, I took a long drink from my rocks glass and anxiously grabbed my phone. It seemed that finding her through social media was the best way to go, and even though I didn't have any personal accounts, the band had several I could use.

I sat at the bar in my basement as I opened one of the social apps and tapped the search bar, typing her name inside it and waiting for the results. But when I scrolled through the list, my stomach sank as none of the faces matched hers.

Damn—I thought her last name wasn't common? I don't even see any Holbachs, though. This sucks.

I closed the app and opened another one, thinking if she had gone into fashion, she'd probably have a profile that focused more on photos than anything else.

Maybe she is an accountant and has nothing interesting to share, so she has no social profiles...

A muscle in my jaw tightened as I thought of her in an office instead of a studio, her dream of design and creativity traded for something that felt safer. When I searched her name again, the results still came up empty, and I squeezed my eyes shut, hoping for *anything* that would make the answer to finding her clear.

Wait... what was her middle name? Maybe she's using it instead of her last name. Crap—I don't remember—wait—

I opened my eyes suddenly, staring at myself shirtless and in blue jeans in the mirrored wall on the other side of the bar.

Marie—Anna Marie—that's it.

I typed it in with a rush of adrenaline, finally seeing her small but unmistakable picture within the first five results. I immediately tapped into her profile and read the bio, which said: *Living the good life in Los Angeles. Lover of faith, fashion, and seafood.*

She smiled in front of a blue wall in her profile picture, and I stared at it as I could hardly believe the truth—that she lived less than thirty minutes away from me.

This is pure madness. How long has she lived in California? Maybe I drank too much and I'm seeing things...

I blinked and reread her bio a few times, but the letters in Los Angeles never unscrambled. I started scrolling through her picture feed, which was full of dresses, food, beaches, and occasionally a picture of her. Anna looked shy in front of the camera; her genuine smile always a little awkward, though her grayish-blue eyes were lively. Her long brown hair was layered and slightly waved, and she had a slender body like I remembered from high school. But despite the passing of seven years, I didn't think she'd aged at all.

Where's a boyfriend? She'd post his picture, right? I'm not going to talk to her if she's dating someone again—though I'm sure that guy in college didn't last. What a stupid interruption.

I downed the last of my drink and pressed the message icon with my thumb, but as I stared at the blank message thread, I realized I had no idea what to say.

This is impossible. I shouldn't say anything no matter what. She probably thinks I'm trash because of the tabloids, which don't print all the facts.

I slid off my stool and walked away from the bar, deciding to forget the whole thing while I hung out in my music room. It was on the other side of the basement, and when I walked through the door, I flipped the light and headed for the large, red sectional in the middle. The walls and ceiling were painted black and mostly covered by acoustic foam, and my guitar collection was mounted to the wall in front of my couch. A short rectangular table sat in front of the sectional, and the acoustic guitar I used to write songs leaned against it. I sat down and pulled the guitar into my lap, but I was bothered by an even stronger urge to message Anna.

Fine—what the hell.

Pulling my cell out of my pocket, I typed a basic message and sent it, then started strumming my guitar.

My notebook laid across from me on the table, and before I knew it, a blank page was covered in lyrics, and two and a half hours had passed. I glanced at the metal clock on the wall, seeing that it was two-thirty. The message I sent to Anna crossed my mind then, and I quickly grabbed my phone, opening the social media app. When I saw a small red dot above the message icon, I tried not to get worked up.

Just another fan message... Anna doesn't care about me anymore.

I nervously tapped into it, overwhelmed by a sudden flood of happiness and surprise when I saw *she* had replied.

ANNA: Hi Adam. It's a surprise to hear from you. We did it!

I grinned and reread her message almost fifty times before I managed to write back.

ME: yeah, we did. it's cool to see all the dresses you've made. if you want, call me.

I sent my number afterward, feeling a tingling restlessness in my body as I wondered if that was the right move. Even though Anna had replied more than an hour ago, I paced the room anxiously as I waited to see how fast she'd get back. It had been a while since I'd been so on edge, and the feeling reminded me of my early fame days, when me, Nate, and Dex started performing in front of thousands. But Anna... she was just one person.

I'm not going to hear back again. She has better things to do than talk to an old crush, even if I'm famous now.

The pressure I felt to accept her rejection vanished when my phone rang a second later, causing my heart to pound inside my ears. I stopped pacing and slowly lifted the cell screen, seeing a local, unknown number. Without a second thought, my thumb pressed the answer button.

"Hey—this Anna?"

"Yes! Adam?"

Her optimistic and energetic tone excited me, the sound of her voice still the same as the last time I'd heard it.

"Yeah! How's the catwalk?"

"I'm not a model," she said with a laugh. "But I do work for Solva and ended up going to fashion school."

"That's incredible—I'm so glad you went for it. I guess I could say things worked out for me too, but I'm sure you already knew that."

"Yeah, I'm so happy for you! How was the tour?"

"Totally insane. We went to big cities all over the world and almost killed ourselves doing it, but the fans were incredible."

"I bet. It sounds very exciting! How does it feel to have everyone know who you are?"

"Interesting and draining, mostly. Do you live in L.A.?"

"Yeah—I've been here for three years. I transferred to fashion school in New York after studying accounting for a year, and all my credits transferred so I still graduated on time. I moved to L.A. after to work for Solva."

"Nice. Why'd you change your mind?"

"I just ended up knowing it was the right thing to do. The more I studied accounting, the more it bothered me, and I finally prayed about it before making the switch."

"Good for you. Your prayers are magic."

She laughed. "I promise they're not, but I do get a lot of guidance through them."

"Whatever you say. But, ah, are you free tomorrow? I live close by in Beverly Hills, and—"

"Beverly Hills?"

I grinned. "Yeah, that super ritzy place. Want to check out my house?"

"Oh—definitely. What time?"

"Whenever you like. If it's before ten, the maid will have to wake me up."

I heard a slight gasp on the other end of the line, and I laughed.

"Kidding, Anna. I don't have a maid."

"Ha—right. I'll be there at noon. I'm still at work, though, so we'll talk again soon, okay?"

"Yeah, sounds good. See you Saturday."

"I can't wait. Bye, Adam."

I pulled my cell away from my ear, hardly able to believe the conversation I'd just had. In less than twenty-four hours, the real Anna would be at my doorstep, her seven-year ghost finally alive in the flesh.

* * * * * *

The next day at noon, I sat on the cement step outside my front door while I waited to see Anna's car pull into the driveway. It was a warm, sunny day—the weather perfectly in tune with how I felt about this seemingly impossible moment. The thought of Anna in front of me was as thrilling as a large dose of blue magic, but unlike that kind of high, I didn't know what to expect as I experienced this one.

I'm not the same as I was in high school—at least, not entirely—and I doubt she is either. She still believes in God, though. I'm not totally godless, but...

Reality faded as all our memories took over my brain again, replaying like the night before while I laid in bed for hours in the dark. Anna's beauty lured me like any girlfriend I'd had, but since our high school days, her faith strangely drew me to her also—even if I couldn't fully understand why.

Her prayers got me to quit smoking, so it has to be real. I'm not an atheist, but I don't know how deep I want to go.

A green Jeep turned into my driveway and I watched as it pulled toward me, then slowed to a stop in front of my garage. The driver's door opened on the opposite side and Anna walked around the back of her car, a wide smile across her lips. A medium-sized tote bag hung from her left shoulder, and she wore a white tank top and cut off shorts, her brown hair loose with sunglasses on top of her head.

"You're not Anna," I blurted, in awe and half joking. "She wouldn't get within miles of a heathen like me."

Anna laughed and rolled her eyes.

"You're not a heathen, Adam. It's great to see you again."

"Same. This feels like a dream, doesn't it?"

"Yeah, but I'm glad today will last a lot longer."

"Me too. Ready to start the tour?"

IMPULSE | Anna

Adam's modern style house in the middle of Beverly Hills was unlike anything I'd seen before as I pulled into his driveway. The house was large and L-shaped, with sections of it made from gray shingles, bright wood panels, and tall panes of glass supported by thick, black metal frames. But I hardly studied it for more than a few seconds before my gaze settled on *him*—his form growing larger through my windshield as I drove closer.

My heart pounded uncontrollably when I parked in front of his three car garage, entirely lost in the fractured reality that started the moment he'd messaged me, and intensified after our phone call. But as nervous as I felt about seeing him after so many years, I couldn't deny that I was equally thrilled.

How can I feel so amazed and terrified? Just take a deep breath and get out of the car...

I grabbed my tote bag from the passenger seat and stepped out, walking around the back of my Jeep to greet Adam on the other side. When I finally had a good view of him, my nerves vanished as a sudden smile spread across my lips. His face was still as young and handsome as I remembered, and he wore a faded gray t-shirt and ripped, dark wash jeans, along with his usual studded belt.

"You're not Anna," he blurted in a joking tone. "She wouldn't get within miles of a heathen like me."

I stood a few feet away and rolled my eyes, at ease as I laughed.

"You're not a heathen, Adam," I assured. "It's great to see you again."

"Same. This feels like a dream, doesn't it?"

"Yeah, but I'm glad today will last a lot longer."

A strong urge to hug him passed through me, and I struggled to ignore it.

"Me too," he said coolly. "Ready to start the tour?"

I nodded, but felt unable to move as my need to embrace him overwhelmed me.

"Wait—I want—shouldn't we—"

The words failed to come out properly as I felt my cheeks burn, embarrassed suddenly by how easily I'd fallen to my impulse. Adam blinked as he stared at me, but thankfully, he quickly figured out what I had tried to say.

"Definitely," he said, spreading his arms. "Come here, Anna."

I smiled and sprung toward him, my arms wrapping tightly around his waist while I pressed myself into his chest. Adam held me firmly as we hugged, and his physical touch caused the fractured reality of our reunion to melt, ridding me of all my shock and disbelief.

It feels right and completely natural to be with him—even after seven years.

A silent minute passed between us before I stepped back, loosening the hold we had around each other.

"I'm ready for the tour," I said happily. "But I had to get that out of the way, first."

Adam smiled with the corner of his mouth, his eyes full of energy that I never saw in pictures.

"Well... if you need anything *else*, just say so," he said, teasing.

I raised a brow at him before we let go of each other and walked through the front door, entering a glass paneled foyer that led into the wide living room. There, three black couches formed a half-circle around the stone fireplace and mounted flat screen, and natural light poured in through several long, narrow skylights.

I followed Adam in awe and excitement as he showed me the typical rooms on the ground floor, then to a hallway with several guest bedrooms, as well as his own at the end of it. When he opened the door, I glanced inside from a few feet away, seeing a gray room with a king size bed and black sheets, as well as scattered clothes and a floor-to-ceiling glass wall with open blinds.

How many girls has he had in there?

"I'll take you to the basement next," Adam said, leaving the door ajar. "It's definitely the best place in the house. There's another living room, a bar, a home theater—"

"What? You have a *home theater?*"

"Yeah, it's pretty cool."

"What's upstairs?"

"Not much. Just an office and small library I never use, and a few empty bedrooms."

"You have a small library? Do you have books in it?"

"I have some books, but I actually put a pool table in there and filled the shelves with a lot of rock memorabilia."

"Oh... that still sounds cool."

"It is. But my music room and home theater are even better."

I smiled. "Okay, let's go."

We left the hall and walked back into the living room, passing the kitchen on the left side as we headed toward an open stairway. It had a thin metal rail and carpeted steps, and mid-way down, the staircase turned one hundred and eighty degrees into the wide open basement.

I gasped silently as I stared at the endless space, which was warmly lit by rows of recessed lights, and had a bar to the far left with a mirrored wall behind it, reflecting the different bottles sitting on top of glass shelves. A large white sectional also sat across from the bar, and the coffee table in front of it had a solid black top, but the bottom was made from a glowing rectangular aquarium. Without seeing his home theater or music room, I already felt deeply impressed.

"It's so amazing down here," I said quietly. "This feels like the perfect escape."

"Exactly," Adam replied, standing next to me. "The rest of the house is pretty standard compared to what I've got down here. Come on, look at the theater room."

I followed him toward a dark wooden door on his left, and we entered a large black room with a projector screen on the back wall, and three rows of reclining seats in the middle. Beneath the screen was a long shelf with countless DVDs on it, and close by sat a popcorn machine, mini fridge, and candy dispenser. A long cushy couch spanned the front wall opposite of the projector screen, and I suddenly imagined lying on it with Adam, his arm around me as we kissed and ignored the movie.

"What do you think?" he asked, breaking my thoughts. "Isn't it great?"

"Absolutely," I said, my cheeks hot. "I'd love to watch a movie in here."

"Sure. Go pick one."

"Oh—not right now. I still want to cook out and go for a swim."

I instinctively touched my tote bag, which held my bathing suit, towel, sunscreen, and a few other items.

"We'll watch one later tonight, then."

I smiled tightly and nodded, though I felt in my gut that would be a bad idea.

We've been together for less than an hour and I already know I can't be alone in the dark with him! What's wrong with me?

"Where's your music room?" I asked, ready to leave the home theater.

"It's on the other side of the basement. Wait until you see my guitar collection."

I left the room with great relief and followed Adam across the basement toward the white sectional, which the door to his music room lay behind. Inside, I saw the twelve unique guitars he had mounted to the wall, and after looking at his private recording booth in the back, we traveled back upstairs to start our cookout.

In the bathroom near the kitchen, I changed into my vintage style bathing suit, which was a floral patterned halter top in navy blue, and matching ruffled bottoms that rose above my belly button. I also grabbed my bathing suit cover from the tote bag and slipped it on, the white crocheted fabric hiding most of my body.

I hope Adam doesn't think I look ugly, but I'm not exactly a string bikini kind of girl...

I left the bathroom and walked to the kitchen, where I agreed to meet Adam afterward. I found him standing between the open double doors of his stainless steel fridge, his bare back facing me while he stood in red swim trunks, his hand wrapping around the necks of two glass beer bottles.

"Want one?" he asked, turning.

Before I could respond, my gaze flashed to his feet and traveled the length of his body, lingering the longest on his lightly-haired chest more than any other part of him.

"Um—no thanks," I managed. "I only like sweetened alcohol."

"Sure, no problem. There's a few strawberry daiquiris in here."

"Who drinks those? Not you, I'm guessing."

"No—they're for guests."

Other women?

I couldn't stop my jealous impulse, but I kept my face calm as I nodded.

"Perfect, I'll take one."

Adam handed me a daiquiri after I walked up to him, and I gazed inside the fully stocked fridge.

"You don't grocery shop, do you?" I asked curiously.

"Hell no," he replied with a laugh. "My housekeeper keeps the kitchen stocked. What do you want to eat?"

"We could make cheeseburgers—and baked beans, if you have them."

"Beans? Maybe. Look in the cupboards."

While Adam took out different items from the fridge, I started searching the cabinets in his large kitchen, eventually finding two cans of maple baked beans and seasoning salt. When I turned back to the island in the center, I saw a pack of ground beef, cheese slices, buns, and an onion sitting on top near my daiquiri.

"Your housekeeper is terrific," I said, placing the cans and seasoning on the island. "I assume you have a grill outside?"

Adam grinned, twisting the top off his beer bottle.

"Anna, I've got everything you could possibly need out there."

He motioned for me to follow as he walked toward the long sliding glass door that connected the kitchen to the backyard and pool area. I quickly grabbed a cutting board next to the stove and piled all our food items on top of it, then crossed the kitchen into the backyard.

There, I saw the inground pool had crystal clear water and a path of white cement bordering it, as well as a small lawn to the far left of it. The perimeter of Adam's rectangle-shaped yard was lined with a tall privacy hedge and black aluminum fence, and between the pool and the house, a row of three reclining sun chairs sat with outdoor cushions. But despite how heavenly it all looked, my jaw dropped when I finally saw his outdoor kitchen built against the side of the house—fully complete with a stainless steel grill, oven, storage cabinets, and mini fridge with a glass door.

"Frying pans, pots, spatulas—everything you need is out here," Adam said, gesturing toward it. "Unless you'd like me to do the honors."

I shook my head, still partly stunned.

"No, I don't mind. I'm an expert at cooking cheeseburgers and baked beans."

"Do you cook a lot?"

"A few nights a week," I said with a nod. "But sometimes I order takeout on the way home."

I walked to the grill and set the cutting board on the counter, then searched one of the storage cabinets for a spatula.

"Where do you live?" he asked.

"I have an apartment in Los Angeles. It's my own perfect escape, like the basement."

After finding a spatula, I tore open the plastic wrap around the ground beef, then glanced at Adam on my right as I started to make beef patties. He had settled into one of the reclining sun chairs, and while he stared ahead and sipped at his beer bottle, I stole another long look at his lean, muscular body.

"I try to do nothing but escape," Adam said after a moment. "Our tour was amazing, but it was pretty difficult, too. I thought Shultz wouldn't plan something so demanding like that again, but I guess he has even bigger plans for next year."

"Shultz is your manager?"

"Unfortunately."

"Did he book too many concerts?"

"Yeah—we did a hundred and fifty shows, and next year he wants two hundred."

"What? How will you have enough time?"

"Don't know. We probably won't go to as many countries, but it's exhausting when most of our concerts last more than three hours. I want to take things easy and enjoy our success now, but Shultz keeps whoring us out."

"You can't control your schedule or get a new manager?" I asked, flipping the beef patties on the grill.

"Yeah, we could, but Dex and Nate don't care what Shultz does. They still want an insane amount of shows like when we first started."

"Oh... I guess there's no way out, then."

"Pretty much. But I've figured out how to survive."

I frowned as I diced the onion, then placed the pieces and a slice of cheese on top of the burgers. After the beans were heated on the stove, I prepared our plates and walked toward Adam, his head leaned back in the sun chair with his eyes closed. There appeared to be no tattoos on him as I studied his form again, and I noticed the dark wedges beneath his eyes were slightly faded in the sunlight.

I sat on the edge of the reclining chair next to his legs, rousing him as I set his plate on his stomach. We started to eat in silence, and after a few bites, I took my first refreshing sip of the strawberry daiquiri. As different topics of discussion passed through my mind, one thing I had thought about since our phone call suddenly came back.

"Why did you reach out after all this time?" I asked curiously. "It really seemed like we'd never talk again."

"A few things happened that made me think about you a lot," he replied after a moment. "I met someone who reminded me of you, and then my mom made a photo collage with our prom picture in it. But I'd always thought about you off and on anyway. Obviously my life has been crazy since getting famous, but right now it just felt right to say something. How long did you date Will?"

My eyes widened at the sudden mention of my college boyfriend, though he had been the reason we'd chosen to stop talking.

"A year and a half," I replied. "It went great at first, but then we realized our goals were too different after I transferred to New York. I tried to call you a while after we broke up, but your cell number was disconnected."

"Really? That must have been after we started getting recognized. Shultz told us to change our numbers for privacy and protection reasons."

"Oh, I guess that makes sense. But you've been busy with your own girlfriends, too."

Adam shrugged, his plate nearly empty.

"Here and there, but no soul mates."

We ate in silence again, and after a few more minutes, we both finished our cheeseburger and beans.

"Ready for a dip?" Adam asked. "It's blazing out here."

I nodded once and smiled, watching as he put his plate on a nearby sun chair and stood, then walked toward the far end of the pool. There, Adam stepped onto the diving board and dove into the deep water, surfacing in the shallow end a few seconds later.

"Come on, Anna," he urged happily. "This feels great! You don't have to be ashamed of your string bikini."

My jaw dropped in surprise and I rolled my eyes, laughing.

"You know I'm not that kind of girl," I replied, echoing my own thoughts from earlier. "I hope my modest suit doesn't disturb you."

After rising, I pulled off my crocheted bathing suit cover and walked to the stairs leading into the shallow end of the pool—all while avoiding Adam's gaze, which had followed me every step of the way. The chilly water caused goosebumps to travel up my legs as I stepped in, and I held my breath until I walked into the middle of the shallow end, where the water line rested just above my hips.

Adam came toward me from a few feet away, the water circling his shoulders as he moved on his knees. I sank down further into the water before he reached me, my lips parting as I gasped quietly, the cool water biting at the more sensitive parts of my skin.

"The chill wears off quickly," Adam said, stopping a few inches in front of me. "And I like your bathing suit. It's cute."

"Hmm. Like what a five year old would wear?"

"No... cute as in fun and desirable. It gives you the right amount of mystery."

I tried not to feel too captivated as I stared into Adam's eyes, endlessly curious and intrigued by the thought of mystifying him.

"Is that... a good thing?" I said quietly. "Offering a little mystery?"

He nodded, a small smile turning the corner of his mouth.

"You'd look good in a string bikini, but then I'd feel like I'd seen it all, and wouldn't have to wonder."

"But doesn't wondering drive you mad?"

"Mad enough to chase after you, maybe."

Adam's face—and his *lips*—were very close to my own, flooding me with a nearly uncontrollable impulse to kiss him. The heavenly sensations of our lips meeting years ago came back to me in an instant, and I relished the memories while my gaze settled on his mouth.

"Do you have a girlfriend right now?" I asked, my gaze flicking upward.

"No. Boyfriend?"

I shook my head, shamelessly stealing a glance at his lips again.

"Adam..."

"What?"

"Could you..."

My cheeks burned beneath the heat of the sun, but also from my own embarrassment as my internal alarm finally sounded. As much as I wanted to kiss him or invite his initiation, I couldn't let myself move that fast.

"...grab some sunscreen?" I finished, though hardly convincing.

"You sure that's what you want?"

"Yes, please."

He raised a brow while his dark green eyes searched mine, and I knew I hadn't fooled him.

MEGA | Adam

The night after Anna's visit, I stared out the windshield of my Range Rover as I drove to a ritzy restaurant in town for a band meeting Shultz had booked in a private dining room. The time had come to officially start planning the next tour, and naturally, I was already in a bad mood about it.

Maybe Nate or Dex will finally say something if he wants us to do two hundred shows or more... but I hate that I can't count on them for it. They still love this insanity—I can't take much more of it. Why can't we do fifty shows and kick back?

I frowned as I slid my hand into my pocket, taking out another small oval of blue magic and tossing it down my throat.

Might as well have a little buzz if I need to go through this. I can't quit the band and hurt the fans. I have to keep going longer somehow...

I fixated on my frustrations until the pressure quickly turned suffocating, causing my thoughts to switch to Anna in an effort for relief. But other than her body having more curves, she hadn't changed much since high school. Her friendly and modest personality was just how I remembered it, and I almost felt certain her religious beliefs hadn't changed, either.

She wanted to kiss me yesterday—even though she denied it. She's probably more into her faith now and doesn't want to give in so easy, but she's my age and dated that idiot for a year and a half... they had to be sleeping together.

The busy streets of L.A. distracted me as I made it through the middle of town and finally pulled into the driveway of the restaurant. I parked in one of the reserved spots at the front and walked in, immediately recognized by the hostess standing behind a long desk in the entryway.

"Good evening, Mr. Avery," she greeted cheerfully. "Follow me to your private dining experience, please."

I nodded once and followed her into the next room, which was small and square-shaped. It had a bar on the left and an exotic tree planted in the middle, and the walls streamed with water that pooled in reservoirs below floor level. I glanced at the seven dark wooden doors dividing the indoor waterfalls, and the hostess led me to the closest one on the right. Inside, the dim, rectangular room had a long table in the center, and a crystal chandelier that hung above it. Despite expecting to see Shultz, Nate, and Dex waiting for me, I felt surprised to see only Nate sitting at the table.

"Where's Shultz and Dex?" I asked quickly.

Nate leaned back with a bored expression, his fingers laced behind his head.

"Shultz went in the other room for a phone call, and Dex had to get Vanessa from the airport, so he'll probably be late."

I walked to the other side of the table and sat down across from him, folding my arms on the surface.

"I guess they're getting serious, now?" I asked.

"Don't know, but I wouldn't let a hot squeeze like that go."

"Hot squeeze? No—what they have is *true love*."

I grinned mockingly at Nate, who smirked back. But before we could say another word, the hostess opened the door, and Dex and Vanessa walked in.

"What are you doing here?" Nate asked, surprised. "You said you'd be late."

"Our driver was positively brilliant," Vanessa answered, her blonde hair falling in waves around her face and shoulders. "He knew how to beat the traffic in town to get us here early."

Her short, mint green dress clung to her body, and her long legs were bare above her black heels. Dex held her hand as they walked to the table, sitting in two of the chairs on Nate's right.

"Perfect! You're all here."

Shultz exited a door behind me, his stern but excited voice filling the room before I saw him. None of us said a word when he sat at the head of the table, looking wolfish and determined like usual, his cell phone just an inch from his hand.

"I did not think a meeting about the next tour would happen so soon," he started. "But nearly all the venues you performed at have offered a twenty-five percent increase in profits if we book now and double our tour dates."

I frowned, my eyebrows furrowing while my stomach twisted.

"Double our dates?" Dex asked, more confused than angry. "We can't do three hundred shows in a year."

"Of course, that's too much," Shultz replied. "The tour would be two years long."

My eyes widened as my heart started to pound.

"Two years?" I blurted. "How is that possible?"

"It's quite possible," he assured, a little annoyed. "Several bands and performers have already done it. The label believes we could easily sell ten million tickets if we announced a two year mega tour, and if so, it would be the highest grossing tour of all time."

"Alright!" Nate exclaimed. "I'm down for it. I want to go back to Germany—they loved us the most."

"Germany was sick," Dex added with a laugh. "We should've let that guy who climbed on stage jam with us before security got him."

"I'm glad you both agree to it," Shultz said, smiling in approval. "Adam, what do you think of this incredible opportunity?"

What do I think? I think you're mercilessly milking us for everything we've got, and it sucks.

I glanced at Nate, Dex, and Vanessa, all of whom had only excitement on their faces.

Why don't the guys want to relax after the last six years? All this performing is killing me, but...

"Sure, let's do it," I said quickly.

Shultz nodded, his smile widening.

"Excellent. You're all smart men. Rehearsals won't start until next December, so you'll have almost a year and a half to enjoy."

He stood and grabbed his cell phone, then walked through the door behind me. Nate, Dex, and Vanessa talked excitedly about the new mega tour while I stared at the table, rubbing the pill baggy between my fingers in my left pocket.

Just a year and a half until my life is hell again? I should have told him I hate the idea, even if it didn't make a difference...

The door to our private dining room opened, and several servers walked in with large circular trays full of different appetizers. While the dishes were placed in the middle of the table, a server with a dark green wine bottle came to each of us, filling our empty wine glasses.

"This ravioli is incredible!" Vanessa praised loudly. "Dex, let's use this place to cater the party."

I watched with mild curiosity as he nodded, biting into half a meatball.

"Adam, will you come to my little fête Friday night?" Vanessa asked, her gaze suddenly on me. "I'm going to live in the states for a while, and I want to celebrate with all my friends on this side of the pond."

I nodded.

"Sure—I'll be there."

Vanessa smiled and squealed, then lifted her wine glass for a sip. I used my free hand to grab my cell out of my pocket and quickly sent a text to Anna, glad for a legit excuse to see her again.

A minute later, my phone vibrated.

ANNA: A party at a mansion? Of course, I'll go.

PARTY | Anna

The week passed quickly while I worked on new dress sketches, making fine adjustments to the Sapphire Nova, and spending almost every minute texting Natalie—who couldn't believe Adam had suddenly reappeared in my life again. Although I could only see her a few times a year when I visited Florida, she was still my best friend, and we frequently scheduled video calls or online gaming dates.

Once I arrived home Friday night after work, I collapsed on the couch and took my cell phone from my purse, reading Natalie's new text message.

NATALIE: Is he on drugs?

My heart skipped a beat as she asked the question I'd secretly tried to ignore... but the truth was obvious.

ME: I don't doubt it. But I don't know what kind, and haven't asked.

NATALIE: You should find out quick. It's cool to see Adam again, but he could have some serious issues.

My nose wrinkled in disapproval, and I tossed my phone a few feet away on the couch.

Do you think I'm a child? Of course I'll find out, but I just reconnected with him. Adam doesn't have serious issues.

The clock on the wall across the living room read ten after six, and I knew I had little more than an hour to get ready and leave for Dex's mansion party. I sighed as I reached for my phone, quickly typing a response to Natalie.

ME: I'll ask—don't worry. But I need to get ready for the party. I'll let you know how it goes.

I put my phone on silent and left it on the coffee table before I walked a short distance to my bedroom. Inside, I smiled at the metallic black dress I'd bought earlier that week as it hung from the top of my closet door. I stood next to it while I undressed, then slipped it from the hanger. After I pulled down the hidden zipper along the right side, I stepped into it and pulled it over my body, then stood in front of the full length mirror attached to my wall.

The collar of the dress tied into a loose, floppy bow around my neck, and the sleeveless top completely covered my chest, while the gently pleated skirt stopped just above my knee. I thought it was a cute party dress falling perfectly between formal and casual, and once I grabbed my matching black clutch and heels, I left my apartment.

The warm evening air glided over my skin as I walked toward my Jeep, and when I sat in the driver's seat, I quickly typed Dex's address into the navigation screen before I started to drive. His mansion was forty minutes away from my humble dwelling, and on the way, Adam's drug problem—which existed to an unknown degree—started to bother me again.

I can see in his eyes that something isn't right, but talking about it isn't as easy as Natalie thinks. Eventually we'll discuss it, but right now... I just want to enjoy being with him.

I bit my lip as memories from the pool returned to me—how good it felt to have Adam so close; how the water slicked his hair back; how perfect he looked under the sun; how drops of water easily slid down his smooth chest...

Why did I hold back? I should have kissed him without letting go... I can't believe I want him so much again...

After reaching Beverly Glen toward the end of the drive, I turned off the main road and onto Cielo Drive, where I stared in awe at the beautifully lit mansions nearby and in the distance. I followed Cielo to a few more back streets before I finally arrived at Dex's mansion, driving slowly through the private gates that stood open.

His house had the same modern, geometric aesthetic like Adam's, and it looked like two perpendicular rectangles stacked on top of each other. His mansion had many large windows, balconies, and outdoor lights, and I parked behind one line of cars on the left of his driveway—immediately noticing the difference between my ordinary vehicle and the luxury transports surrounding it.

Why are so many people here already? Hopefully no one calls a tow truck...

I climbed out of my car and walked alone toward the front door, though I could easily hear music, voices, and laughter from around the side of the mansion. A small keypad was next to the golden, horizontal handle, but the door swung back effortlessly as I pushed against it.

I immediately walked into a large room full of people, and the entire bottom floor was almost visible from where I stood. The living room, dining room, and kitchen were a length apart but sat in the same open space, and the left wall had a seamless line of sliding glass doors that led to a wide balcony with a stunning view of hills and other incredible mansions.

I waited by the door as I searched the crowd for Adam, but I was soon approached by a tall, beautiful blonde woman. She wore a red lace dress and had her hair pulled back into a large braid, and I felt that she might be part of the fashion industry like I was.

"Hello!" she said in a lively British accent. "You must be a guest of my guests."

I smiled shyly and nodded.

"I am—I was invited by Adam Avery. What are you celebrating?"

"My move from England to the states! I'm Vanessa Holt."

"Oh, nice to meet you. I'm Anna Holbach and I work for Solva fashion," I replied.

Vanessa's eyes widened with intrigue, and I felt glad I followed my instinct.

"Brilliant! I've been a model for years and have worked with Solva a few times back home. What do you do?"

Before I could answer, she motioned for me to follow as she walked away from the door.

"I'm a concept designer, so I create gown ideas for their collections. My latest one—the Sapphire Nova—was chosen for their fall collection next November."

"Really? Fantastic. You have pictures, don't you?"

"Of course."

Vanessa led me to the balcony, where I saw Adam and Dex standing in a group next to the railing. When we joined their circle, I stood next to Adam, his face immediately brightening while his arm slid around my shoulders. He held a martini glass in his other hand, and I could tell by the glassy look in his eye that he'd had a few drinks already.

"Hey, you. How's it going?" he asked.

Adam's lips spread into a charming smile, and I quickly admired his polished outfit, which consisted of a black and gray plaid blazer, a white button up shirt, and black slacks.

"Terrific," I said with a smile. "I was just about to show Vanessa the dress I designed for Solva's fall collection next year."

I opened my black clutch and took out my cell phone, showing both of them several pictures of the Sapphire Nova.

"Absolutely beautiful," Vanessa said, swooning. "When is the collection debut? I want to see it in person if I can."

"I'm not sure of the date yet, but I'll have you added to the guest list."

"Excellent. Now, how do you know Adam?"

"High school," he cut in. "But we just started talking a little bit ago."

"We were enemies at first," I said with a laugh. "But then we worked on a project together and went to prom."

"Oh... enemies to lovers? Quite delightful."

A surge of blood warmed my cheeks, and I couldn't help the thought that immediately came to mind: *We're not lovers, yet.*

"How do you know Dex?" I asked her.

"I met him backstage while they all toured Europe this summer," Vanessa replied warmly. "And now that we're exclusive, I'm going to model here for a while—perhaps indefinitely."

"You need a drink," Adam suddenly suggested to me. "Come on. The food is good inside, too."

I nodded once and smiled at Vanessa, then followed Adam across the balcony once his hand slipped around mine. The electric feel of his skin thrilled me, and a chill raced down my spine as I focused on the warmth and firmness of his grasp. While we walked through the house toward the kitchen, my eyes darted to every closed door—wondering if any of them could comfortably hide us away from everyone else.

Stop it. Why can't I act normal? We can't be alone and risk breaking my boundaries. He needs to woo me and be a gentleman—like Will—but I...

Adam stopped in front of the long marble island in the kitchen, my gaze sweeping over the multiple food spreads and bottles of alcohol on top of it. He grabbed the top of a toothpick that pierced an olive and a few slices of cheese and meat, then pulled it clean between his teeth.

"Are we friends to lovers?" he asked.

My surprise nearly made me speechless.

"I don't—I don't know."

"You wanted to kiss me in the pool. Why didn't you?"

I blinked, my mouth falling open for a second.

"Adam—I… I just met you for the first time again in years that day."

"So? It's not like we haven't kissed before."

"Seriously? You should know I don't move that fast."

"I actually don't know anything about you anymore, but I bet you want to kiss me now."

My surprise only increased, and as hesitant as I was to confront his drug habit or explain my dream, one or both seemed to be the only option at hand.

"I can't talk about this right here," I said, my gaze flashing to the crowd near us. "Let's go to a private room."

I grabbed his hand and Adam followed me wordlessly from the island toward a closed door. After opening it, I found a spacious room on the other side, with a mostly empty bookcase and a desk pushed against the wall without a chair.

"We can talk in here," I said, pulling Adam inside with me.

I closed the door and faced him, my heart pounding heavily against my chest. He stood a foot away from me and waited, his eyes still glassy, and his intoxication broken enough to be patiently curious.

"You know I'm still a Christian, like I was in high school," I admitted. "But as an adult, I've taken my faith a lot more seriously, and I…"

My voice stopped, like a defense mechanism for one of my deepest desires—which so few had understood.

"What? God doesn't want you to kiss me?"

"No—it's not that. I just… I have boundaries, Adam, and I can't move fast in a relationship. There are certain things I want that aren't so popular anymore."

My body was immediately covered in sweat as if I had actually confessed my choice of abstinence before marriage, but I hardly had a moment to think about saying it plainly before Adam stepped forward, brushing the back of his fingers along my jaw.

"You're still beautiful," he said, his voice low. "I always thought you were pretty in high school, and the last night we spent together before graduation, I thought you were the most beautiful girl I'd seen… I guess that hasn't changed."

His words passed like a strike of lightning through me, and I wrapped my fingers loosely around his wrist while Adam cupped the side of my jaw.

Just do it—kiss him! I can't resist now, I can't—

I closed my eyes and leaned into him, but this time, Adam's lips quickly met mine. Our mouths met and separated feverishly at first, until his lips locked with mine and his tongue ventured into my mouth. Before I knew it, my back was pressed against the door, and I pushed Adam away the moment I had the strength to leave such an exquisite heaven.

"Happy now?" I asked, fighting a smile. "I did want to kiss you Saturday, and I don't regret doing it now. But we have to slow down, Adam."

"Did you sleep with Will?" he asked.

I furrowed my eyebrows, confused and unexpectedly annoyed.

"Why does that matter?" I countered. "Whether I did or didn't doesn't change how I feel right now."

Adam frowned as he stepped back, and I sighed while trying to catch my breath.

"I think there's a lot we need to learn about each other before something like this happens again," I insisted. "We should probably go out to dinner or something and... talk."

I thought he would agree right away, but Adam's expression darkened until he shrugged. He stepped toward me and grabbed the door knob, causing me to move aside quickly. When he left, I stared after him, upset that our glamorous evening had just ended.

BLIND | Adam

I woke up the next morning on my living room floor, my head pounding as I stared at a crumpled blanket between me and the couch. No clear memories came to mind while I laid there, but eventually, I tried to lift myself up slowly.

Dex... his party... no, Vanessa, her party...

I managed to stand for only a second before collapsing sideways into the couch, longing for an aspirin bottle while I squeezed my eyes shut. I still wore the same clothes from last night, and despite my head throbbing, pieces of Vanessa's party started to come back.

Anna, she was there... and we... did we...?

With my eyes closed, I saw us standing alone in a room at Dex's house, talking and also kissing. I imagined moving her back against the door, her arms around my neck while I deepened the kiss to feel the inside of her mouth.

No... it didn't happen... the stuff I snorted is making it seem real...

The fantasies of me and Anna faded into real memories of a room where I'd sat with Nate and a bunch of other people around a table covered in all kinds of illegal paradise. At some point last night, I'd gone to the top floor of Dex's house and snorted two rows of something I'd never tried before, and after that—I couldn't remember much else.

Anna already left... early... don't know why...

I finally forced myself off the couch to slog to my bedroom, where I yanked a drawer open in my bathroom and grabbed an aspirin bottle. After swallowing four pills, I pulled off my clothes as I walked toward my bed and climbed into the sheets. The comfort of my pillows and mattress was a rare dose of lawful happiness, and I knew I'd be asleep again in minutes—hopefully for hours.

* * * * * *

The clock on my nightstand read 3:03pm when I woke up again. The throbbing in my head was gone as I stared at the ceiling, still unable to remember the drive home, or how I ended up on the living room floor.

Damn it—how many memories got erased from snorting? I don't even know what that stuff was...

My mind felt lost in grogginess until I thought about my car and suddenly sat up, not knowing how I'd parked or possibly damaged it. I slid my legs over the side of the bed and staggered into the hallway, wearing only my boxers as I headed to the front door. In the driveway, I saw my Range Rover parked halfway on top of a tall bush next to the garage with the driver's door hanging open.

What the hell? Why don't I remember this? Idiot!

A small dark shape on the concrete a few feet away caught my eye, and after walking toward it, I found my wallet lying closed on the ground.

Great. Wait—my keys—where?

I scooped up my wallet and walked to the open driver's door, where I looked inside a few seconds before I noticed a sour smell. My nose wrinkled as I stared at the leather passenger seat, which had chunks of food and dried puke juice all over it.

Why can't I remember this? This is insane! How did I make it home?

I saw the key fob in the center cup holder and climbed inside, firing the engine and backing the SUV off the bent bush. After parking in the garage, I went back inside the house to get dressed and grab a few cleaning supplies. Even though I could hide the accident and puke explosion from my housekeeper, Nina, before she came back on Monday—I wouldn't have time to fix the smashed bush.

It's fine—I don't need to fix it. I'll say Nate drove here drunk and hit it. She'll never know the difference.

✸ ✸ ✸ ✸ ✸ ✸

I stared blankly at the large flat screen over the fireplace while I laid on the couch a few hours later. The memories of the party before Anna left had all come back, and I knew the fantasies I'd had of kissing her actually did happen last night. But as much as I enjoyed thinking about it, I remembered her suggesting a dinner out to talk—to come clean about whatever it was that bothered her.

She's obviously seen the tabloids. Probably thinks I'm a heroin addict or something. All I really like is my blue magic, and I should stick to it since I don't wind up passing out on the living room floor...

My gaze dropped from the black screen to my phone, which laid in front of me on my stomach.

I should call her... but I don't need to say anything about the pills. They're not dangerous like snorting, and I'm never going to do that again. Anna couldn't understand the kind of pressure I'm under with the band. She doesn't know what it's like to be buried in other people's expectations...

I sighed and reached for my cell, frowning as I remembered—*again*—leaving her in the spare room after she stopped kissing me.

She won't answer if I call. She shouldn't. I was terrible.

Despite my better judgment, I tapped her number a few seconds later and brought the phone to my ear. It rang several times, then, surprisingly—

"Hello?"

"Oh—uh—hey, Anna."

"Hi, Adam."

"How are you?"

"Good... you?"

"Fine. I'm sorry if last night sucked. Usually the parties I go to are a lot more fun."

Anna didn't respond right away, and I raised a brow, waiting.

"I liked the party, but I don't know why you got upset and walked away from me."

"Yeah, I'm sorry, that was stupid. I just—I didn't want to talk about the tabloids right then."

Anna sighed faintly on the other line, her complicated struggle easy to sense.

"I wasn't trying to talk about anything right then, but... what are you doing tonight?"

"Come over tomorrow morning and I'll take you to a private beach in Malibu," I replied quickly. "It's the perfect place to relax all day and swim in the ocean. We can talk about anything you want there."

"Oh, well... okay."

"The beach is downhill from a mansion owned by a music exec I know. She lets me or the guys hang out there when she's out of town."

"Sure, that sounds great."

"Perfect. Come at ten, then."

"Okay. Bye, Adam."

I pulled the phone from my ear and ended the call, slowly filling with pride and relief.

The beach was a great idea—whatever she's heard about me, this will show her my better side. I can make her have the time of her life with hardly any effort. What other guy can do that?

I got up and grabbed my key fob on the coffee table, believing an expensive gift would help with any truths I might have to admit to tomorrow.

No one is perfect. Not even her.

BEACH | Anna

While I drove to Adam's house the next morning, I started to wonder how much longer I could hold on to my dream. For the last five years, I had easily guarded it from the world, but now... the pressure of losing my virginity without a vow weighed on me far more than it ever had. I'd fallen for Adam just as quickly as I did years ago, and even though I worried about his reported drug habits, I didn't want to let it—or *myself*—stand in the way of our second chance.

When I pulled into the driveway at his mansion, I saw Adam loading a large cooler into the back of his SUV. He wore a tropical print shirt that hung open down the middle and light blue cut off shorts. I smiled at his unusual outfit and parked beside the Range Rover, then walked around the back of the Jeep toward him.

Like my first visit, my tote bag hung over my shoulder, but my normal clothes were tucked inside as I'd decided to wear my bathing suit and crocheted cover-up instead. My hair hung in a loose braid over my right shoulder, and like Adam, my sunglasses were pushed back on top of my head.

He turned from the cooler and grinned after I stopped next him, his gaze quickly sweeping from my head to my feet.

"You went straight for the kill," he teased. "I thought you'd change at the beach mansion."

I smiled and shook my head.

"I wanted to be more efficient, but I'd still love to go inside."

"No problem," he replied, closing the hatch door. "I've packed all the drinks and food we're going to need, so let's go."

* * * * * *

The sun shined brightly and warm air passed by the open windows while Adam drove us along the eastern Malibu coast.

I leaned my head back against the headrest and gazed through my purple-tinted sunglasses, hardly able to understand how such a plain and silent moment between us could be so perfect. The radio played quietly while I studied the lines of Adam's body—the ridge of his nose, curve of his lips, length of his throat, grooves of his chest and stomach—which I caught glimpses of while his unbuttoned shirt flapped around in the gentle breeze.

I was right to hold out all those years, but now... everything is different. I have another chance to explore love with him, and if Adam was the first, I don't think I could regret it, not for a second...

My gaze drifted passed Adam into the sparkling ocean beyond, its white-capped waves rising and falling slowly in the distance.

Whatever problems he has can't be that bad. I prayed for him to stop smoking in high school, and I'll do the same thing again. I know he needs me.

I smiled a little and closed my eyes, turning my head back toward the windshield. Eventually, we left behind the smaller homes and businesses on the coast and pulled into a gated community off the main highway.

Adam stopped the Range Rover in front of a long black gate, and the guard inside the security booth confirmed his access before we drove through it. The spotless paved road beyond was long and winding, and the mansions we passed were massive, spread out, and few. But the ocean seemed to shine more beautifully here than it did in public territory, and after almost ten minutes, Adam finally turned into the driveway of the music executive's mansion.

The front was shaped like a horseshoe with a three car garage to the left, the large front door in the middle, and other rooms filling the right side. Its clean white exterior and black shingled roof looked elegant, but its decades of age stood out from the modern builds around it. A granite, flowing fountain with statues of dolphins and mermaids sat in the middle of the driveway, and Adam parked to the right side of it, then pressed a button that automatically opened the rear hatch door.

"The front of this place isn't so impressive—wait until you see the back," he said excitedly.

"Are you kidding? I'm impressed!" I said with a laugh. "That fountain is incredible."

We climbed out of the SUV and I helped Adam carry the large, heavy cooler to the front door, where he punched a code into the keypad beneath the handle. We then stepped inside the foyer, which had dark solid wood floors and tall, white walls with crown molding. The rest of the house followed this design as we passed through it, and most of the furniture looked like one of a kind antiques, though still useful and comfortable.

Adam led me through the wide living room toward a large sliding glass door and several windows with an incredible panoramic view of the Pacific. Once we passed through the sliding door, we crossed onto a wooden deck that spanned the length of the house, and had a beautiful wrought iron rail with scroll decor. I gazed at the forever unreachable horizon line where the ocean met the sky, and glanced at the other mansions and their private beaches that sat a comfortable distance away.

"Any more impressed?" Adam asked.

I smiled shyly, nodding.

"It is amazing out here. I can't wait to take a dip in the water."

Adam turned and led me toward his end of the deck, where we carried the cooler down a flight of stairs onto the green lawn. We followed the land's gradual slope toward the beach, and once we stepped into the sand, we walked several yards before picking a spot to make ourselves comfortable. After I let go of the cooler, I opened my tote bag and spread my beach towel on top of the sand in front of it. Adam pulled his towel off his shoulder and laid it next to mine, his hands on his hips as he turned toward the ocean.

"Nothing beats this," he said happily. "I need to buy a house here soon."

"What's it like being a millionaire?" I asked eagerly. "One of the best feelings in the world, right?"

Adam shrugged.

"It's not bad. It felt amazing at first, and still does... but after a while, you realize there are still better things out there."

"Of course," I said with a nod. "Money isn't everything, but if I had millions of dollars, I would want to live here, too."

Without another word, I slipped off my crochet cover-up and started jogging toward the ocean. Adam's heavy footsteps soon struck the sand behind me, and I ran a few inches into the water before I suddenly jumped back out of it.

"It's like an iceberg!" I shouted.

Adam laughed, standing a few feet in front of me in the water.

"You'll be fine once you go numb," he insisted. "Come on—I thought you wanted to take a dip."

I shook my head and stepped back further, but to my horror, Adam rushed toward me. I stood paralyzed in shock until he scooped me in his arms, then carried me quickly back into the ocean. While he waded deep into the water, I clung to his chest with my arms wrapped around his neck, the icy waves causing goosebumps to rise across my skin.

"You're going to pay for this," I scolded.

"Yeah? What's the punishment?" he replied, smirking.

I frowned and tried to look threatening until a large wave crashed into us. Adam's hold around me tightened until the force of the water passed, and I hardly had a moment to think before the second wave struck. My body felt thoroughly chilled when the ocean calmed, and while Adam laughed, I pushed free of his hold, sinking my feet into the soft sand a few feet away.

"Good thing I didn't wear makeup," I said in a fuss. "Clearly I had no choice to stay dry."

Adam smiled proudly while he pushed back the hair in his face, the perfect lines of his body melting my annoyance without effort.

"Don't complain if you won't do anything about it," he said, his tone challenging. "If you want to punish me—I'm ready."

I raised a brow and grinned, slapping my hand in the water to splash him. Adam immediately dove into the water, and a few tense seconds later, I felt his hands grab at my legs like a sea monster. I laughed and tried to move away, but when he surfaced, I pressed myself against him and put my hand over his mouth.

"I'm not going to kiss you again if we're just friends," I said gently. "*That* is your punishment."

Adam lifted his eyebrows, the curious look in his eye seeming to hold an endless list of questions. I removed my hand while my body shivered against him, though I knew it wasn't because of the frigid ocean.

"Since we agreed to have a serious talk... I slept with Will."

Adam blinked and nodded once.

"It doesn't matter," he said quickly. "And I didn't mean to ask like that. I'd had a few drinks and when you said we needed to slow down... it just came out."

"Why?" I countered. "You said it didn't matter."

"It doesn't. But when you said you had boundaries, I wasn't sure if it was because of your religious beliefs."

I shook my head, causing a deep stab of pain to spread across my chest. Despite how much I wanted to confess my dream and reasons for it, I couldn't bear to have Adam look at me the way Bristol, Maggie, and everyone else did. From him, it would finally be too much.

"It's not," I managed. "I just didn't want to rush into anything at the party—it wasn't the right place."

"Yeah, I guess it wasn't."

My gaze shifted from his while shame consumed me, and Adam started walking toward the beach.

"Ready to warm up in the sun?" he asked.

I followed him wordlessly out of the water and across the sand, then settled into my towel next to him. We sat close enough to nearly touch, and Adam opened the cooler behind us, taking out two bottles of alcohol.

"It's your turn," I said, trying to keep my tone light. "I haven't made any serious assumptions, but the tabloids—"

"They're liars," Adam said quickly. "I mean, obviously I tried a few things at the beginning of my career, but I'm not doing anything anymore."

Adam put the cold strawberry daiquiri in my lap and turned again, rummaging through the duffle bag that he'd dropped next to the cooler. While I hesitated to ask what kinds of drugs he'd tried, a small white box appeared in front of me in his palm.

"I wanted to get you a gift," he said, smiling. "I hope you like it."

I raised my eyebrows and took the box carefully. It hardly weighed anything, and after pulling off the top, I saw a gold bracelet lying on top of a folded square of white satin. A small gap prevented the top of the bracelet from joining in the center, and the left end was fashioned into a leopard's head. Its eyes were small emerald gems, and white diamond fragments dotted its back like natural spots. The right end of the bracelet narrowed like a tail, and every part of it shined brilliantly under the sun.

"This is—I've never seen—"

"It's very special. Don't be scared to try it on."

I blinked and glanced at Adam before I cautiously reached into the box, wishing I could somehow touch it without leaving a mark. I pressed my fingers together and slipped them through the bracelet, letting it slide down my wrist as I tilted my hand upward. The cool metal briefly shocked my nerves until it warmed against my skin, and I felt in my gut that it had been wildly expensive.

"Is it real gold?" I asked.

Adam nodded. "Most of it. Real emerald and diamond shavings, too."

"How can I accept this? It's so nice—"

"Don't worry about it. I definitely didn't go broke. I'm hoping you'll wear it to the Viva Rock Awards with me next week."

My jaw dropped as I stared at him.

"Are you sure I'm the right kind of date?"

"Why not? You'd look good in a leather dress."

My surprise melted as I rolled my eyes, and Adam smirked.

"Maybe I should take another girl," he added quickly. "I need a fearless rock goddess."

I raised my eyebrows, smiling slyly at his challenge.

"As long as I can look classy, you will have no finer goddess than me."

Adam gazed into my eyes for several long seconds before he leaned into me. I almost lost my ability to breathe when his mouth stopped an inch from mine, and his left arm crossed over me, his hand resting on my hip.

"No kissing if we're friends," I said in a desperate whisper.

"We're not friends, Anna."

I blinked, my heart pounding.

"I know."

His lips met mine as I closed my eyes, and I laid back against the towel, my arms wrapped around his neck while half of his body covered me.

LIES | Adam

Me, Dex, and Nate sat in a private suite at a Los Angeles club while downing shots from a long flight of tequila. We were above the main dance floor, and spinning lights flashed in and out of a line of windows to our left, which looked down onto the crowd. Nate and Dex sat across from me on another couch, and hanging at the club had been Dex's spur-of-the-moment idea.

"We're going to get Record of the Year Friday night," Dex said excitedly, knocking an empty shot glass off the table. "That's the little secret I wanted to share. Someone from our label told me, but I *swore* I wouldn't say who."

"That's it?" I replied, rolling my eyes. "I thought it was already obvious."

"Yeah, we're the most popular band nominated," Nate added. "Of course, we're going to win it."

Dex frowned, his expression disappointed.

"Sales count just as much as popularity," he said defensively. "A lot of press doesn't always mean you're the best sellers. The Jaded's newest album hit platinum five days before ours did—*five* whole freaking days. If they'd kept that up, we wouldn't have won."

"Damn! I guess they need Shultz to book a few soul-sucking tours—seems to work perfect for us."

My body quickly grew hot as I stared at the mostly empty shot glasses on the table, avoiding the gazes of Nate and Dex.

"Why does it bother you so much?" Nate asked, annoyed. "We're going to have one of the greatest tours ever next year. Who cares how insane it is?"

"Because Shultz isn't doing this for us or the fans—we're just his money machines. I mean, we just toured for a year, and now he's already planning the next *two years* of our lives with *another* tour. What if I want more time off? Or what if our next album bombs because of the tight timeline he's got going for us? I know why he booked us like crazy in the beginning—but now it's pure control."

I finally shot a glance at Nate and Dex, their expressions twisted like I'd just spoken Chinese.

"That's not true," Dex said plainly a second later. "We all agreed to it the other night when we met with him. You should have said something if you didn't like it."

I swallowed another shot of tequila before dropping the empty glass carelessly on the table.

"Nothing I said would've mattered," I replied. "You guys wanted to do it, so why try?"

Nate snorted and rolled his eyes while Dex shrugged.

"Seen Anna since the party?" Dex asked.

I nodded. "We hung out at the private beach in Malibu this weekend."

"Really? Bet that impressed her. Is she still a Christian?"

"Yeah—I'm going to ask her out after the Viva Rock Awards."

"You are? Does she know you're an addict?"

I shook my head, and Dex laughed.

"Don't you think she'll be upset about that little secret?" Nate asked.

I looked away from him and shrugged.

"Does she even get down and dirty?" he continued. "You know, Christians aren't supposed to be like that."

"She slept with her college boyfriend," I countered. "I'm not worried about it."

"Anyone else?" he pressed. "She graduated how long ago?"

I furrowed my eyebrows, frowning.

"What are you getting at? You think she's lying about having sex?"

Nate shrugged, and I didn't like the amused smile on his face.

"Maybe not, but wouldn't it be funny if you were both lying to each other? I mean, if Anna is still a good Christian girl, I'm sure she'll be happy to blow out your candle."

While he grabbed the last shot of tequila and drank it, I angrily stood and left the room. My feet stumbled from all the alcohol and blue magic in my system as I walked down the dimly lit hallway, but eventually, I turned into an empty unisex bathroom. There, I pressed my back against the door, trying to calm down while my blood pressure soared and my vision stayed blurry.

Anna isn't a liar. She's not terrible like me, and I'll tell her the truth, just not yet...

I took a few deep breaths, realizing the pill and tequila combo had done practically nothing to help me into a good time that night. Instead, I just felt angry and sick.

She wouldn't lie about sex, because even if she's a Christian, she still lives in the same world we all do...

My knees and feet started to feel numb, and a minute later, I slid onto the floor in a sitting position, my legs stretched out in front of me. Even though it was hard to focus on anything other than my nausea, I decided I didn't care what Nate or Dex thought about Anna.

She won't love me if she knows the truth... but I'll tell her... eventually...

I managed to smile a little while memories from our perfect day at the beach played in my mind without order. It was the best day I'd had in a long time, and eventually, my head dropped forward as my eyes closed. The memories turned into life-like experiences as the minutes passed, but my dreams scattered when I quickly woke up to a sour feeling in my stomach.

I crawled weakly toward the toilet and threw up into the porcelain hole, the bathroom filling with a strong acidic smell while I imagined the nightmare of Anna seeing me now. But I was surprised when the door suddenly opened, and Nate and Dex stepped in with confused expressions and wrinkled noses.

"We were worried about you, man," Nate said, staring down at me. "Why didn't you say you felt sick?"

"I wasn't sick," I replied, turning from the toilet as I sat against the wall. "I just needed to cool off—then this happened."

"Listen, we're going to talk to Shultz about the tour," Dex said eagerly. "He probably should back off a bit. We can tell him we don't want anything longer than what we just did."

I blinked a few times in shock, though it barely cleared my vision.

"Thanks, but don't let the dream tour go because of me," I replied tiredly.

"Come on, Adam. How are we supposed to do any touring if you're like this?" Dex asked, his tone agitated. "You need to slow down with the pills."

I shrugged as I closed my eyes again, but Nate and Dex grabbed me by the arms and pulled me from the floor. It was easier than I thought to stand on my own two feet, and I staggered slightly as I followed them out of the bathroom.

"Let's go to another club," Nate suggested to me and Dex. "This one is too boring for my taste."

"I'll drive," I offered, digging into my pocket for my keys.

"Don't think so," Dex replied. "Give them to me or buy a coffin."

I blinked and furrowed my eyebrows.

"Seriously? You guys go then. I'm going home."

"What? Adam—"

"You don't need to control me, okay?"

I glared as I turned away from them, walking the opposite direction down the hall.

RED | Anna

I need to be on birth control...

That strange, foreign thought had been circling my mind since our day at the beach, where I'd lied and became someone I didn't know.

I stood alone in my bedroom while I stared into the full length mirror on the wall, waiting to see through my skin and into my soul—to figure out how much longer I could deny myself for Adam. Three days had passed since our trip to Malibu, and the nearly excruciating pain of my lies hadn't gone away.

We are more *than just friends... I believe we're meant to be together... but like this? And I'm not actually his girlfriend, right?*

After we kissed on the beach, Adam and I talked for a while about easy and lighthearted things—but neither of us questioned what our truthful yet unclear agreement of being "more than friends" meant. My gaze narrowed as I stared at my reflection, suddenly disgusted and fascinated by how quickly I had abandoned the most significant pieces of myself to win him—and all without his knowledge or persuasion.

He doesn't dream of the same things I do—he can't even understand them. Adam won't love me if he knows the truth right away, so I have to hide for a while before I can come clean, unless...

I finally looked away from myself in the mirror as a new, strange thought came to me. But I hardly had time to consider it before I heard my cell phone ringing in the living room. I left my bedroom and walked to the couch, where I sat on the middle cushion in front of the coffee table and grabbed my phone. Natalie was calling, and before I answered, I took a deep breath and hoped I wouldn't have to tell her anything that had been on my mind.

"Hi Natalie," I said, slightly anxious.

"Hey! How are you?"

"Um, good. You?"

"Fine. I finally watched that space movie you like. I still can't wrap my head around the fourth dimension."

I smiled and managed to forget my worries while we discussed intergalactic travel and dimension hopping—something we both hoped would be possible one day. But when we shifted to our daily lives, my heart pounded when my best friend asked about Adam.

"Did you find out if he's on drugs?" she asked curiously.

"Yeah—he said he wasn't. I mean, he admitted to trying a few things a long time ago, but the press still writes that stuff about him."

"Why doesn't he look very healthy in photos then?"

"He's tired of touring so much," I said quickly. "His manager is a control freak and doesn't ever let them have a break, but there isn't much he can do about it."

"I'm sure that's part of the problem," Natalie said, unconvinced. "But I did some digging a few days ago, and I read an article that just came out after the tour where he admits to using narcotics."

I could almost feel the blood drain from my face, and I tried to ignore how incredibly foolish I felt instead of surprised.

"What article?" I asked quickly. "He just told me on Sunday that he wasn't doing anything."

"It's from Tumble Rock magazine, and he said, 'The amount of shows we do is crazy, but I have some magic pills that keep me going.' Anna, I don't think it gets any plainer than that, and I don't know why he'd lie about it when all you have to do is a quick internet search."

My mouth fell open to respond, but no words came out as my thoughts froze for a few seconds.

"That quote sounds like he's joking," I said in weak defense.

"I doubt it," Natalie replied. "What are you going to do about it?"

"Um... I don't know. He asked me to go to the Viva Rock Awards with him Friday night, and I'm really excited about it."

"Do you think he's going to ask you out soon?"

"I don't know. When we hung out in Malibu on Sunday, we agreed we were more than friends, but... we didn't actually say if we were dating."

"Oh, that's interesting. I don't think you should date him though, since, you know—he lied about using drugs."

I squeezed my eyes shut and took a deep breath, my own lies preventing my anger at Adam from boiling over.

"I guess he's getting what he deserves, then," I confessed resentfully. "He doesn't know how I really feel about sex, and I'm not going to tell him until we spend a lot more time together. I'm afraid he'll just treat me like everyone else if he finds out too soon."

"Wow—really? I mean, I understand that a little, but he's not really getting to know you then. Doesn't it sound like you're tricking each other?"

I blinked and frowned, the truth of her words causing my stomach to feel sick.

He thinks I slept with Will when I've never been with anyone... but he decided to trick me with a lie, too.

"Maybe he's doing that to me, but what if I don't have to?" I said thoughtfully. "I've been happy to save myself for the right person... and if that's Adam, then maybe I can relax a little. Maybe I don't have to wait for the ring on my finger. If he's the one, then it really doesn't matter when we sleep together."

"Are you serious?" Natalie replied after a moment. "The ring is what proves your feelings aren't fooling you! Do you know how many people give everything they have to someone and end up heartbroken when the breakup they never imagined happens? Come on, Anna—you know this."

"That's true," I replied defiantly. "But I am a twenty-five year old woman, and maybe it's time for a change, anyway."

Natalie's end was silent for a few long seconds, and I waited with hardly any regret.

"Wow... I'm really not sure what else to say," she finally said. "You don't sound like my best friend at all."

"It's okay, Natalie. I'm just trying to figure things out right now. I love every minute I spend with Adam, and I don't want to go years without seeing him again."

"Okay, well... good luck with him."

"Thanks," I said quickly. "We'll talk later."

"Sure. Bye."

After the line went dead, I dropped my phone in my lap and leaned back heavily into the couch. Natalie—who'd married Jake two years after high school—simply had no way of understanding the situation I was in. And the black and white answers she gave to me that once seemed so clear were now lost in endless shades of gray.

• • • • • •

I left work early Friday afternoon and drove to a VIP salon in downtown L.A. called Marcelles, which sat in the middle of a plaza that attracted the richest clientele. The salon was in a narrow brick building with several stories, and Adam had told me to meet him there so that a team of stylists could prepare us for the award show.

I felt a whirl of butterflies in my stomach as I entered the double doors and stepped into the ground floor lobby. A receptionist sat behind a wooden desk with a black granite surface to my left, and after checking in, I learned Adam was in suite nine on the third floor. The shiny silver doors of the elevator were at the end of the lobby, and when I stepped inside, I pressed a white circular button with a black three on it. While the elevator slowly rose upward, I took a deep breath and closed my eyes.

I can do whatever it takes to make us work. I hate that I lied to him, but he did the same—I read the article for myself. Oh well. It's not like he's on heroin or LSD or something... he probably lied because he felt the same way I did.

The elevator chimed as the doors rolled open, and I immediately snapped out of my thoughts as I felt surprised to see Adam walking down the hall toward me. His lips curved into a handsome smile, and heat rose into my cheeks as I stepped out to greet him.

"You're early," he said. "I was just going down to wait for you."

"I couldn't wait to get here," I admitted. "This place is so chic and cool."

"Yeah, it's nice. Ever had a team of stylists work on you?"

I rolled my eyes, laughing.

"What do you think? I'm just an ordinary person, unlike you."

Adam raised a brow, his left hand gently gripping my chin.

"I've never thought of you that way. Come on—I'll introduce you to the beauty crew."

I never thought I could feel so confident while staring into the black lenses of countless paparazzi cameras.

Two elegant braids on either side of my head led back into a high ponytail, and my false lashes, gray eyeshadow, red lipstick, and bronzer made me feel glamorous. I wore a black leather dress that covered my chest and shoulders, and it reached the middle of my thighs, high above my mid-calf leather boots. The expensive leopard bracelet also dangled around my left wrist, and I held a black clutch in both hands.

Adam stood beside me on the long red carpet, his arm resting comfortably around my waist while we posed for the cameras.

"Who's the girl?" a photographer shouted.

"Adam! New girlfriend?"

"What's your name, honey?"

"She's a new face! Actress? Model?"

My eyes flashed to Adam as I wondered what we should do, but he seemed to read my mind as our gaze met.

"Don't worry about what they say," he said, his quiet voice close to my ear. "We just need to look good for a few minutes and then we can go inside."

I nodded and tried to smile happily into the cameras again until Adam guided me away with gentle force. The red carpet led to a long white tent with enclosed sides in front of the award show theater, and inside the tent, Adam grabbed two glasses of champagne from a passing waiter and handed one to me. The tent was full of people drinking and talking, but so far, I didn't recognized any of their faces.

"How's the star treatment feel?" he asked, taking a sip.

"It's unlike anything I can imagine," I admitted, also swallowing a little champagne. "I loved being beautified by the style team at Marcelles—I'm going to miss that."

We walked through the tent and into the theater building, where we passed through the lobby and into the event hall. The dark walls were brightened by many lights in the arched ceiling, and countless round tables were covered in gold cloth with floral centerpieces and silver plates. The wide stage at the opposite end of the room was dramatically lit, and Adam led me to a table where Nate, Dex, and Vanessa were already waiting.

"You went to Marcelles, didn't you?" Vanessa asked us immediately.

"We did!" I said, grinning as I sat next to her. "Where did you go?"

"Ugh—it doesn't matter," she said with a dramatic sigh. "You are *so* beautiful and I look like complete *rubbish*."

Dex, who had been listening, quickly put his arm around her as she frowned.

"You're hotter than ever, Nessa," he assured her. "Next time I'll book Marcelles in advance."

A pleased smile spread across her lips before she kissed him, and despite her disappointment, few women looked more beautiful than she did that night. My gaze drifted to the centerpiece, and while I studied the short bejeweled vase full of small white roses, Adam's hand suddenly squeezed my knee.

"You know, we're winning tonight," he said quietly. "We've got the biggest award—Record of the Year—in the bag."

My jaw dropped as my eyes widened.

"What? How do you know?"

"Someone at our record label told Dex, but it's not a big surprise. I already assumed we'd win."

"Oh, I mean, you are one of the biggest bands out there. Is it still exciting?"

"Definitely. But we have to sit through this whole thing until we get called up at the end."

"I don't have to go, right?"

My heart pounded at the thought of having millions of eyes on me during the broadcasted ceremony, but Adam shook his head.

"No. You can stay with Vanessa."

I sighed in relief and pressed my hand on top of his, thankful to avoid a second set of cameras that felt much more intimidating.

We then talked to Vanessa and his band mates, and almost twenty minutes later, the lights dimmed and music gradually filled the event hall. The stage was brightened as a host walked out and officially started the award show. During his introduction, waiters appeared silently out of the dark and surrounded our table, setting down plates of grilled chicken, vegetables, and salad.

We ate while the first few awards were announced, and I couldn't help the strange sense of alarm I felt when Adam excused himself to the bathroom. But it grew as I repeatedly glanced at his empty seat.

Is he leaving to take pills, or some other drug? But why am I worrying about this? Of course he's just going to the bathroom like he said—even if he lied to me. He doesn't need to go to the bathroom to get a fix... right?

I finished my plate a few minutes later and leaned back, trying to laugh at the jokes the host told before congratulating another award winning band. But after what felt like fifteen minutes of Adam being gone, I could hardly focus on anything else.

Get a grip—he's not doing drugs. Maybe his stomach got upset, or—he bumped into someone and they're talking right now. Yeah, that's probably it. Everyone knows who he is and he got caught up talking on the way back...

I took a deep breath and crossed my legs, my left foot twitching nervously as it hung in the air. Eventually, I tried to glance around for Adam in the dark, but all the eyes facing me quickly made it feel awkward.

When another five minutes passed, I finally decided to search for him, but Adam appeared suddenly and slid down into his seat. My tense muscles immediately relaxed as I stared at him, though his face was mostly turned toward the stage. While my mind felt overwhelmed with too many questions, I thought Adam seemed as calm and relaxed as he was before—except for a quiet sniffing noise he made every five or so seconds. And for the next thirty minutes, I sat in painful silence until the nominees for Record of the Year were announced.

"Many bands had great success this year, and although a few were neck and neck at the top of the charts, only one has been chosen for Record of the Year," the host announced grandly. "Now take a deep breath and prepare to scream for... REBEL RIOT!"

The room erupted in applause as the lights brightened and celebratory music played. While everyone in the event hall stood, clapped, and shouted their congratulations, Adam turned toward me. His droopy eyelids made him look tired, but I saw with dread the bright red rim of his left nostril.

"I'm so g-glad you're here, Anna," he said, his excitement breaking through his sedated tone. "I wanted you here tonight, because I w-want to say... I love you."

TRUTH | Adam

Anna stared at me in shock, though her face wasn't entirely clear as the world around me was blurry. I followed Nate and Dex from the table to the stage, but my legs felt mostly numb, and I jerked up my hand to rub my itching nostril.

The bright lights pointed at the stage hurt my eyes while the three of us walked across it toward the waiting host, but despite the pain, I smiled and laughed at nothing specific. The host held a shiny silver guitar that was five or six inches tall, and after he spoke to the crowd—saying something I couldn't focus on long enough to understand—he handed the silver guitar to Dex, who then took the mic.

"We're amazed and thrilled," Dex said happily. "It's good to be home after touring so many other countries, and Record of the Year is a terrific accomplishment. We thank the committee and most importantly, our fans."

I grinned and nodded quickly as I stepped behind Dex and wrapped my arms around his shoulders, hugging him tightly from behind.

"We won!" I shouted past him into the mic. "We knew t-t-tonight would be amazing—that we—we're the b-best—!"

My arms dropped as Dex suddenly shook me off of him, and I felt Nate grab my left arm and squeeze it hard.

"What the hell?" he whispered loudly. "Act normal, man. We're on live TV, remember?"

I started laughing and tried to smack his hand off my arm, but I wasn't sure how long it was before Dex grabbed my other arm and they pulled me forward across the stage. I stumbled down a few steps that looked like a solid black mass and easily ignored all the faces that stared at me while my best friends led me back to our table. The room was blurry, dark, and slightly spinning, but I felt a little better when they pushed me down into my chair.

"Adam! What's wrong?" Anna asked.

I grinned and ran a hand through my hair, then let one arm hang over the back of my chair.

"Nothing, b-babe—I *love* you."

I wanted to say it a million times, but before I could, Anna sighed heavily.

"The ceremony is almost over—just sit still and don't say anything."

Her worried expression seemed ridiculous to me, and while I managed to stay quiet, my left leg bounced uncontrollably. Anna sighed again, and I quickly grabbed her hand and squeezed it.

"Don't worry, b-beautiful—we won."

When the ceremony ended a half hour later, my high finally started to disappear. I hadn't snorted a very large hit in the bathroom, but it was enough to make me soar for almost an hour afterward.

The world wasn't blurry anymore once the lights came up in the event hall, but I still felt pretty careless while Nate, Dex, Vanessa, and Anna all stared at me in the suddenly loud room. I shrugged and waited, unsure of what really bothered them.

"We're going to be in all the tabloids for that, Adam," Nate informed. "Shultz is going to lose his mind."

"We're already in all the tabloids," I replied lazily. "Who cares if I'm having a good time? Just tell Shultz I was drunk."

"That isn't going to help," Dex said, frowning. "Do whatever you want, but I can't believe you got high right before we were called up there. You made us look stupid."

I shrugged again and played with a fork between my fingers, but Anna grabbed my hand and stood up.

"We need to go somewhere and talk," she said. "Everyone around is staring at you."

"Fine—but I don't care about them."

Her mouth formed a thin line before she turned away, and my legs felt a little more steady as I followed after her. Almost every table I passed mentioned my name, but I didn't look at anyone as I focused on Anna, who led me into an empty hallway with a lot of doors. She walked toward the first one in front of her and peeked inside the room, then went in. I walked into it slowly and shut the door, seeing the large space had a few windows and was being used to store furniture, boxes, and stage equipment.

Anna stood in the center, her eyes locked on me while she managed to look sad and angry.

"Why are you doing drugs?" she asked immediately. "You have everything a person could ever want, but you're okay with risking your life?"

"Wait a second—that's not what's happening," I replied casually. "I don't overdose and I don't take anything that messes me up for days. I know exactly what I'm doing."

Hearing my own words had me convinced, but Anna made a skeptical noise and rolled her eyes.

"You really know what you're doing? Then why did you get high before accepting your award?"

"Stop acting like what I did up there was terrible," I said, annoyed. "So I acted a little goofy—big deal? I didn't make us look stupid."

"You lied to me, Adam," Anna shot back, her tone upset. "You said at the beach the tabloids were wrong and you weren't doing drugs anymore. I can't believe you did that!"

Her breathing quickened as she stared at me, her face and neck turning slightly red. I frowned and reached for her waist, pulling her a few inches closer to me.

"Anna, I didn't want to lie," I replied, my carelessness slipping into anxiety. "I just wanted you to know me first—to *love* me."

Her hands squeezed my wrists as she sighed, and her breathing grew more controlled.

"Why should I fall in love with someone who is destroying himself?" she asked quietly. "Don't you see where this is going? So many people die because of their habit, Adam—not to mention countless musicians."

Anna's gaze fell from mine as her face tilted toward the floor, and her breathing picked up again as she started to cry.

"Anna, don't. Relax, it's okay—"

"It's not okay, and it's not only that. I lied to you too, and I can't pretend anymore."

My eyes widened in shock, though I felt extremely confused.

"You lied?"

"I never slept with Will. I only said that so you wouldn't think less of me."

Anna's gaze met mine again, but this time it was filled with pain and tears.

"You know I'm a Christian, Adam, and since high school, I've only taken my faith more seriously. Sex is special and sacred to me the way God intended it, but when I tell people that—or that I'm saving myself for marriage—they think I'm strange and naive."

My heart pounded as she pulled herself forcefully out of my hold, covering her face with her hands as she cried freely. I stood frozen for what seemed like far too long, but when I finally stepped toward her, Anna pushed my hands away.

"Don't say anything," she said quickly. "I can't imagine you would think any different after what I know about you now. Clearly sex, drugs, and rock n' roll is all you want. I need to get out of here because I can't stand the thought of you treating me like everyone else."

Anna turned for the door, but surprisingly, I couldn't make myself go after her. My body felt like it was made of cement while my brain scrambled to sort out a flood of emotions that threatened the last of my high. Though my mouth fell open as Anna left the room, there was nothing I could say to change her mind.

●　●　●　●　●　●

I stared at the ceiling while lying in bed early the next morning. My mind was in a fog from being awake for many long, dark hours, and I convinced myself again that Anna had paid a cab to get her home last night—that she didn't have to walk the streets of L.A. all alone without my limo.

I sighed and closed my eyes, my thoughts shifting to everything else that happened before she'd left. My actions had been less than stellar, and Shultz would definitely be on me for it—but Anna had confessed her own lie, which Nate had suspected to some degree.

Part of me felt like I should have known, but I was still shocked.

Anna is a virgin... it's what she wants before marriage... but she didn't want to tell me... I could have guessed, maybe, if I wasn't in denial...

I rolled onto my side and buried my head beneath a pillow, trying hard to understand her feelings when my own virginity had never been so precious. But eventually, I understood her in a small way—how she might want to save some of those first thoughts, touches, and vulnerabilities for someone who didn't have an expiration date. Most of the world didn't see it that way anymore, though.

She doesn't want me to treat her like everyone else, but honestly...

I groaned, feeling buried by the same weight of torn emotions I felt last night after the ceremony.

...I don't know what to do.

● ● ● ● ● ●

When I didn't hear from Anna by the mid-afternoon, I finally decided to call her. I sat at the edge of my pool with my feet in the water, listening to her end of the line ring several times, though it didn't seem like she would answer. Of course I wanted her to, because even though I'd told her I loved her while high, I'd meant it, and wanted to talk more about her way of seeing things.

After the sixth ring, Anna finally picked up.

"Adam? I'm surprised you called."

"Hey, Anna—sorry. I would've done this sooner, but I barely slept last night and feel like trash. Did you make it home okay?"

"Yeah, I used a cab."

"Good. I figured you did."

Heavy silence fell between us, and after a few awkward seconds, I didn't know what else to do other than blurt out my thoughts.

"I've never thought of sex as sacred—special, yeah, sometimes—but I've never heard of it the way you have. I get why other people don't understand, but I don't think you're strange or naive. I can see how it's part of who you are, and I'm not going to treat you bad about it."

Anna's end of the line stayed silent, and impatience ate at me while I forced myself to wait.

"That's great, Adam," she replied, sounding relieved and almost breathless. "I don't want it to be a weird thing between us, and I can't tell you how many people think I'm hopeless for ever finding true love. That always hurts and makes me feel like who I am isn't enough… but I believe for the right person it will be."

"Definitely. It's just that once you have sex, you want more, and that's the problem for me and everyone else. A lot of people aren't raised like you, so we try things and have to keep going. It becomes another means of survival—like food, water, and air."

"I understand," Anna said at length. "And I don't want to wind up in the same position. It's one of my dreams to save sex for marriage, because I always want it to be incredible and exclusive—but that's difficult when sex is everywhere, and the pressure to have it is extreme. No matter what everyone else is doing, I just can't imagine treating that bond so casually."

When she finished, I said nothing as memories of my hook up with Ava in London came to mind. I couldn't have treated sex any more casual than I did then, and though that night had already haunted me, I knew it was one I never wanted Anna to find out about—mainly because I started to feel the shame in it.

"I see your point," I replied quickly. "But I also want to say that I'm sorry for how I told you I loved you. I didn't mean for it to come out when I wasn't thinking straight—but I do love you, Anna. When I said we were more than friends at the beach, I meant it."

My heart pounded during my confession, but instead of Anna feeling happier or excited, she sighed.

"When will you stop taking drugs?" she asked seriously. "I'm glad you accepted my truth, but like I said last night... I can't be with someone who is foolishly risking their life."

"But I'm not doing that," I said, trying to hide my annoyance. "Yeah, I do some stupid things sometimes, but I would never take enough to kill myself. That's ridiculous, Anna."

"It's really not," she snapped. "I'm actually ashamed of you, Adam. Stop acting like people don't accidentally overdose or take something that's lethally laced. Along with sex, I can't understand why people treat drugs as if they're no big deal."

"Do you think I'm an idiot? Whatever I snort or swallow helps me deal with the miserable tours Shultz always makes for us, and he's done it for the last six years. I've tried talking to Nate and Dex about doing less shows, but they don't care that we're his money machines. In fact, Shultz is already planning our most demanding tour next year, and I'm never going to make it out alive if I stop using."

My expression twisted angrily as I stared into the pool water. Anna's know-it-all attitude was insulting, and truthfully, she knew nothing about that side of my life, or what it took to perform on stage every day for hours on end. I thought her delayed response was because I'd proven my point, and I started feeling satisfied.

"Last I checked, your tour ended weeks ago so you shouldn't have gotten high last night, but I don't want to fight about this," Anna replied, her voice tired and distressed. "If you don't want to stop… then I think we need a break from each other."

"Seriously?"

"Yes. I can't stand by and wait for the worst to happen—whether you believe it will or not."

"What are you saying, then? We're not going to talk or see each other again?"

"I'm sorry, Adam. I can't say for how long, but I have a lot on my mind and I don't see myself fitting into your life right now."

A muscle in my jaw tightened as her words echoed in my head, and I tried to convince myself that she wasn't being completely serious.

"If you need time… take it," I replied. "But everything is going to be fine—you'll see."

"Okay, well, I need to go."

"Wait."

The line was silent while the chilling emptiness of her absence already started to creep through me. But as much as I didn't want any space between us, I couldn't turn away from the mega tour, or what I had to do to get through it. The pain of losing her for a second time created a heavy weight on my chest I'd never felt before, and it seemed to be the first of many ways this moment would go on to crush me.

"Nothing—nevermind. Bye, Anna."

"Goodbye."

FIVE MONTHS LATER

CALL | Anna

"Want to get something from that vendor?"

I looked down the left side of the street where Zach pointed after we stepped out of the movie theater. Not far from us, a snack and hot dog vendor was serving another couple, and I nodded at him, eager to fill my stomach with more than the two buckets of popcorn I'd had during the movie.

"So, on a scale of dumb to incredible—what'd you think?"

I furrowed my brow thoughtfully as we walked a short distance down the sidewalk, trying to analyze the whole film in a matter of seconds.

"It was right in the middle—decent," I replied. "The plot was really good, but the characters could have been better. I felt like they weren't that interesting."

"Yeah, I can see that. I wish I had a '69 Charger like they did, though. I physically felt pain when it crashed."

I laughed as I smiled, and when we reached the vendor a moment later, Zach and I ordered two hotdogs. He stood a foot taller than me and had dark brown hair that matched his eyes, and along with a handsome face, he also had a laid back personality that I enjoyed. I'd met him a few weeks ago at church, and during our first date last week, I found out that we had quite a bit in common—too much, almost.

We walked across the street afterward and sat inside his car, but while we ate our hotdogs, my thoughts gradually drifted to Adam. I hadn't heard from him since our last phone call months ago, and other than his behavior at the Viva Rock Awards, nothing had been reported about him—which I hoped was a good sign. But I had no way to know for sure, and despite often wondering about him, I still felt determined to keep myself distanced.

"If you knew someone with a drug problem, it would be smart to keep your distance from them... right?"

Zach blinked as he looked at me, my serious question suddenly breaking our silence.

"Probably," he replied. "But it depends, I guess. Do you know someone like that?"

"Yeah. He's... a long time friend, but I quit talking to him a while ago because I can't watch him hurt himself."

"Oh, I get it."

"What do you mean it depends, though?"

"If the person is a family member, you probably shouldn't distance yourself."

"Okay. He's not."

"It's your call, then."

I nodded, and once we finished our hotdogs, Zach drove me back to my apartment complex. We agreed to another date as he walked me to my door, and after I hugged him goodnight, he disappeared down the flight of steps that led up to the third floor.

I unlocked my door and stepped inside once he was gone, tossing my purse on the couch as I walked toward the bathroom. While I washed my face and began the rest of my nightly routine, my thoughts were still sliding back to Adam, and for the first time in five months, I started to doubt if cutting off contact had really been the right choice. I sighed heavily as I stared into my own eyes in the mirror—depressed and hardly surprised by their sudden dullness.

I thought I could stop loving him if we stayed apart, but... did it actually work?

I squeezed my eyes shut and pressed my palms against them, trying to make sense of my new, carefree affection for Zach and my intense, long-held desire for Adam. It didn't seem possible that I could want both of them—two exact opposites—at the same time, and as much as I hoped that someone like Zach would make my feelings for Adam seem totally crazy, I couldn't ignore my urge to finally reach out to him.

After shutting off the bathroom light, I walked back into the living room and took my phone out of my purse, quickly pulling up Adam's contact profile. But instead of tapping his number right away, I stared at it as my heart began to pound. There was no telling how he felt about me five months after I severed ties, and it was entirely possible he'd managed to write me off as easily as I did him.

Or... tried to.

I took a breath and closed my eyes, attempting to work up enough courage to dial.

Just call. If he doesn't want to talk, he won't answer, or call back.

Without another thought, my thumb pressed his number, and my heart continued pounding as I put my phone to my ear.

What are you doing? Hang up!

Despite the horror of not knowing what to say if he answered, the line kept ringing, and eventually, I got his voicemail with a sting of disappointment. I ended the call without leaving a message and sank down onto the couch cushion, feeling even more confused about our situation than I had before.

I called too late—I should have waited until tomorrow.

I sighed as I glanced at the clock hanging above my TV, which read 10:03 p.m. I left the living room and walked into my bedroom, where I set my cell phone on my dresser before I changed into pajamas. But just as I reached for my phone to take to bed, it started to *ring*.

I stared in shock at Adam's name on the screen, and after two rings, I immediately answered.

"Hello? Adam?"

"Hey, Anna—it's Dex."

My brow furrowed as I tried to make sense of hearing his voice instead, and I didn't like that he sounded worried.

"Dex? Where's Adam?"

"He's in really bad shape right now. He got in a car accident last night, and the doctors aren't sure what's going to happen."

My entire body went numb as his words instantly pierced my core, causing a level of panic to rise inside me I had never felt before.

"W-what? Dex—wait—are you being serious?"

"Dead serious. Can you come?"

* * * * * *

Walden-Crosse hospital was a twenty-five minute drive from where I lived, and each minute felt like the last Adam would have before he died.

I drove robotically along the interstate highway while cruel, fear-fueled images of his bloody and broken body being pulled from his car filled my head—convincing me that he would die before I could make it to him. When I finally parked in front of the hospital, I walked as fast as I could to the front desk, where Dex had a nurse waiting to escort me to where he, Nate, and Adam were on the tenth floor. After an elevator ride and several long corridors, the nurse joined me with Dex, who stood beside a room that the nurse walked into and shut the door.

"Tell me everything!" I said in tears. "Is Adam in there?"

"Yeah, he's all hooked up to machines and wrapped in casts and gauze. He drove off the road into a ravine after we left a friend's house in the mountains last night—Nate and I were behind him and saw the whole thing."

"I bet he was drunk and high, right?"

The distraught look on Dex's face intensified.

"I didn't want to let him drive," he confessed. "But he's been bent out of shape about not talking to you and we didn't want to make it worse."

You did make it worse! He's practically dead!

I sighed heavily and gripped the bridge of my nose with my thumb and index finger.

"Where's Nate? Are Adam's parents here?"

"Nate and Vanessa went to the cafeteria, and his parents aren't here yet. They're both out of town and trying to get here. His dad lives in Wyoming."

"How bad is he injured?"

"He's definitely got a few problems, like brain swelling and a broken pelvis. His left leg is also fractured, and he's having some breathing issues. It's a good thing you called, because I wasn't sure what to do. Adam made it seem like you guys would never talk again."

I bit my lip while too many complicated and painful feelings flowed through me to explain what had happened to Dex, but we were distracted when the door to Adam's room suddenly opened. I watched the nurse step out, her eyes on a clipboard as she walked away down the hall.

"Can I... go in there?" I asked, almost afraid.

"Sure, but he's not awake," Dex replied, disheartened. "The doctors had to put him into a coma."

The sting of tears came as I turned away and wrapped my hand around the door knob to Adam's room. I opened the door slowly and stepped inside the dimly lit space, which felt like the size of two rooms instead of one. The back of his bed was pushed against the far left wall, and a bright, narrow light lit the room above it, for the large ceiling lights were switched off.

While I walked toward his motionless body, an immediate sense of his identity was obscured by thick layers of gauze that covered his eyes and most of his head. Adam wore a standard hospital gown and a nasal breathing aid, and several IVs and other thin tubes were attached to his body from multiple machines. His hips lay inside a pelvic cast that also extended down his left leg, and a long translucent tube filled with blood came out of his right side. His arms were relaxed at his sides, and when I stood beside his bed, I carefully laced my fingers through his, the warmth of his skin bringing unexpected relief.

"I shouldn't have tried to block you out, even if I was afraid for you," I said quietly with regret. "I should have stayed to tell you to get help a million times and watch over you. I'm so sorry."

My vision blurred as a few tears broke loose, but I took a deep breath and quickly wiped them away.

"I should have told you I loved you when we spoke on the phone months ago, but I hope you already knew that."

Adam lay still with no hint of response, and I sank into the chair a few inches behind me, my right hand still holding his. For the next while, I sat beside him and stared at the visible lower half of his face, praying silently that he would fully recover from whatever injuries he faced, and that his flat, lifeless expression would forever disappear.

When I finally decided to leave, my body felt heavy like lead as I tried to stand again.

"I have to go home, but I'm watching over you now. I'll be here every day until they wake you up."

● ● ● ● ● ●

Two long and hard weeks passed before Adam's doctors decided to bring him out of his medically induced coma. Solva had managed to keep me busy enough to stay sane, and after some thought, I decided to stop seeing Zach. But on Adam's first day of consciousness, I drove straight to Walden-Crosse after work.

Dex, Vanessa, and Nate had already seen him earlier that day, and when I arrived at his corridor, I was surprised to see an older man outside his room that had a striking resemblance to him. The man sat on a bench across the hall in a polo shirt and dark jeans, and he held a newspaper and a cup of coffee. His sandy brown hair was the same natural color as Adam's, and the shape of his rounded face also looked similar. Before I could think, he glanced over at me, and I smiled a little.

"Here to see Adam?" he asked gently.

I nodded as my cheeks grew warm.

"Yes... I'm Anna Holbach. We've been friends since high school."

"Oh, your name sounds familiar. I'm Lee Avery, his dad."

My eyes widened, though I felt I should have assumed as much.

"How is he doing?" I asked with concern.

"Good. He still has a long way to go, but he woke up well this morning. I was in there a while ago, but he's been dozing in and out from the pain medicine."

My pulse raced at the thought of looking into Adam's eyes and hearing his voice again, for after the tragic accident and such a long absence from him, that basic form of connection seemed painfully impossible.

"That's good to hear. I want to go see him, but I won't disturb him if he's sleeping."

"Don't worry about that—I'm sure he wants to see you."

I sighed quietly and walked a short distance to his door. I opened it slowly and stepped inside the room, which was bright from the ceiling lights and the open blinds of the large rectangular window. Adam lay still on his bed like normal, the gauze that had covered his eyes and head for weeks now gone.

I struggled to stay calm as I walked to his bedside—feeling nearly overwhelmed with nerves and excitement—but Adam didn't move or open his eyes when I stood beside him. For several long minutes, I stared at his pale, emotionless face, and watched his chest rise and fall gently.

I smiled and reached for his hand, hoping that the feel of my fingers between his would rouse him. Within seconds, Adam's head moved slightly, and his fingers twitched.

"Adam... it's me, Anna."

He opened his eyes slightly, and although Adam didn't respond right away, his hand closed around mine.

"I'm glad... you're here."

His soft voice startled me, though I quickly recovered.

"How do you feel?"

"Don't feel much... just tired."

"If you need to sleep, please do. I'm so glad you're alive."

Adam closed his eyes, and I wasn't sure how soon he would speak again, but—

"Anna... I want you to know... that I believe in God."

My eyes widened as I stared at him, thankful that he wasn't looking at me at that moment.

"Oh—that's fantastic, Adam."

"I wanted to tell you... but even with you... it was hard."

"Why?"

"Because... I'm not a very good person."

"Of course you are," I replied gently. "You've had some deep struggles, but that doesn't make you bad."

"You... were right to leave me. I was so stupid... and now... look."

I sighed heavily as tears stung at my eyes, feeling little pride in my predicted outcome of his drug abuse.

"I wasn't right to leave you," I confessed. "I should have been checking in on you, and praying for you at least—but I didn't even do that."

A few cool tears touched my hot cheeks, and I wiped them away while a question came to mind.

"When did you start believing in God?"

"About a year after I came to California," he said at length, his eyes half-open. "Because when we got famous... I knew he'd heard me."

"Heard you? When?"

"High school. I said... if I came to California and made millions... I'd believe in God, like you. It was a joke, but then... I did."

"Wow, that's incredible, Adam. I'm glad you told me, because I believe God saved you from dying. Your injuries are bad, but it seems like you'll recover fine."

"Yeah... we'll see."

We fell into silence for a short while after that, and I focused on the feel of Adam's warm hand against my skin—a welcome sign of his regaining liveliness and health. But despite my apology for abandoning him in a desperate time, there was yet another thing I had to come clean about—though it would be a much happier confession.

"You said you loved me, and I love you, too. The first time I felt it was when we left the white bridge on prom night, and those feelings have been getting stronger ever since we reconnected. I thought I could stop myself from loving you by shutting you out, but it didn't work. I called your phone the day after your accident to see how you were doing, and that's when Dex told me what happened. But starting now, I'll be your girlfriend, and help you in whatever way you need."

When I finished speaking, my body felt strangely light. I saw a faint smile grow on Adam's lips, though he had closed his eyes again during my speech.

"Glad to know," he replied quietly.

I smiled and settled into the chair at his bedside, watching over him silently as he fell back asleep.

WORST | Adam

I didn't have any memories of the accident when I woke up from the coma. All I could clearly remember was the party me, Nate, and Dex had been at before it happened, and the loud sirens of the ambulance while I lay in the back on a stretcher.

But the morning I was conscious again, Dex and Nate told me how I'd driven off the road into a mountain ravine as they followed behind in another car. I'd gone to the party an hour after they did because I didn't want to go at first—but I'd been depressed and alone for almost two weeks, and eventually decided to go out.

Even though I was upset they'd let me drive after how high and drunk I was, I knew how much I must have fought them, and the cost of my recklessness was extreme: brain swelling from head trauma, a broken pelvis, fractured leg, and a collapsed lung—not to mention several cuts, bruises, and other minor injuries.

Thankfully, the pain medicine I was on dulled any serious pain, but the minor, constant aches I had still almost drove me mad.

During my first day of consciousness, I hardly had a second to think about Anna as I tried to make sense of everything around me and the result of my accident, but when she'd been at my bedside that evening, I felt more strength than I expected to push through and recover.

For the next three months, I was bed-ridden in the hospital, and the day I was released, Shultz and my parents had arranged for me to go to one of the top rehabs in California. The program was two years long and required me to live on site for the first six months in lockdown, though I could have visitors in the evening.

I sat alone on my bed journaling one afternoon during my second week there, as my therapist told me it would be an easy way to see changes in myself over the next six months and track my goals.

The accident is the worst thing I've ever been through, but it's caused a lot of good changes.

One, Anna—my long overdue girlfriend—is back in my life again, and two, I'm finally going to start making better life decisions...

Also, Shultz still wants me to do the mega tour when I get out of here, but I

> *still don't want to do that many shows. I don't see how I can if I want to avoid my "triggers" for drug use, as they call it here.*
>
> *But anyway, Dan wants me to come up with some goals before our therapy session today, and so far I've come up with two big ones, which are...*

I quickly finished my journal entry and tucked my notebook under my mattress before I stood up carefully. Despite the break in my left tibia healing well, I had a lot of scar tissue and permanent nerve damage, which caused major pain to shoot through my leg if I put pressure on it too quickly.

The room I lived in had a bed, window, wooden wardrobe, a small bathroom and kitchenette, and even though it was all nice—I still felt like I was in some kind of prison. I walked slowly out of the room and turned right down the hall toward the elevators, which would take me down a level to the counseling offices on the second floor.

My therapist Dan—or Mr. Morris—was a relaxed guy in his fifties who seemed to genuinely care about me, and I never felt scrutinized while talking to him. We'd already had two sessions my first week, and although I could talk about anything, we agreed to always keep an on-going conversation about my triggers and how to overcome or avoid them.

When the elevator stopped at the second floor, I stepped out and walked a short distance to Dan's office, feeling nervous to tell him about the goals I'd set. Though they were serious and achievable—possibly—like he wanted, I still wasn't sure if one of them was too extreme for a recovering addict.

After I pushed open his office door, Dan smiled at me from behind his desk, his expression always happy and friendly. I smiled back as I walked across the room, sitting down on the red couch along the left wall.

"How are you today, Adam?" he asked, his tone light and energetic.

"I'm kind of nervous," I admitted. "I thought of some goals I really want... but I'm not sure if they're too much."

Dan raised a brow and laughed.

"Oh? What are they?"

"Well, the first one is about Anna. One of her dresses is going to be in a fashion show a few weeks after I can move back home this fall, and I was thinking—if I was doing great and it still felt right—I would propose to her the same night."

Dan stared at me in surprise for a second before he nodded his head, but that was enough to make my anxiety spike.

"Is that insane?" I asked quickly. "I mean, you know how far back we go and what we've been through. Does every messed up addict you talk to want to get married?"

"Certainly not," Dan replied humorously. "But a few do, however. I think that is a worthy goal, but a strong marriage will require a lot more than successful treatment here."

"What do you mean?"

"We give the help and skills you need to stay clean and avoid your triggers, but a marriage must have two people willing to put their spouse ahead of their own needs. Some people are naturally suited to that kind of service out of love, and others struggle a great deal. It's something you will have to learn about yourself, and make adjustments as necessary for the benefit of you and her."

I blinked as I thought about his words, realizing how clearly they described my feelings about the proposal—even though I couldn't have explained it half as good.

"I think I can do it," I replied thoughtfully at length. "Even though the accident was terrible, it's made me want to take life and the people I care about more seriously. Marriage wouldn't have been something I wanted before—especially at twenty-five—but I've seen how short life can be, and there's no reason I can't give Anna what she wants. I love her and she dreams about things like this."

"Very well," Dan said, satisfied. "The perspective you've gained will definitely enrich your life from what it was before, and the more you do for your loved ones, the happier you'll be."

"What about tough sacrifice?"

"It's true that not every act of loving service is without pain, but it all works toward a long term, happier outcome. As long as you keep that in mind, you can't go wrong."

"That's good. Anna doesn't want to have sex before marriage because of her beliefs, so it's something I have to give up for a while."

"Well—that's very considerate of you. I'm sure Anna will appreciate that more than you'll ever know. You said she is a Christian?"

"Yeah."

"Are you?"

I raised a brow while a small smile turned the corner of my lips.

"The worst one, I'm sure."

Dan's serious expression vanished while he laughed.

"Keep that humility. I think almost every true Christian would say that about themselves, but patients with faith affiliations have very high recovery rates after rehab. Now, what was your second goal?"

I swallowed hard as my anxiety ate at me again, and my gaze dropped from Dan to the floor.

"Shultz still wants me to be part of the mega tour," I confessed. "But since I can't do a lot of walking or standing without ridiculous pain, I think he'll finally listen to me about cutting back on our tour dates."

I waited for Dan to agree, but after a few seconds, I glanced at him and saw his serious expression.

"Performing stress is your greatest trigger for drug use," he said, concerned. "Even if your manager listened, it's probably best to step back from it altogether."

"And what—quit the band?" I asked, my tone upset. "I don't know if I can do that. I started it with my best friends, and the thought of walking away for any reason kills me. I only stress out about performing when Shultz makes a suicidal schedule, and if I can't physically do what he wants, then he'll *have* to make changes."

Dan sighed a little while I stared at him confidently. Finally, it seemed like I had won the war with Shultz and the mega tour.

"Use the next six months to focus only on your recovery," he replied steadily. "Your total wellness and staying alive should be your top priority."

RING | Anna

I never imagined being the girlfriend of a rock star in rehab—but since the first day we met, Adam had always led my life to unexpected places.

During the six months he lived at the rehabilitation center, I visited him several times a week, and we usually made dinner in his room or walked the beautifully landscaped grounds together. Although Adam wasn't allowed to leave the property in an effort to keep him fully immersed in his recovery, it was rare that we wanted more than our own conversation, and a number of long, deep kisses.

As time passed, I learned that Adam's journey to stay clean of drugs and handle the pressures of his career would be lifelong, but despite the gloomy shadow it cast, I didn't doubt our destined futures.

When I wasn't with him, I spent the rest of my time preparing for Solva's fall fashion show that would feature the Sapphire Nova and Bristol's dress, the Dawn Frost, among several others. And because it had been impossible to hide that I was seeing someone from her, I had to continually dodge Bristol's questions about his identity—which I promised she'd find out the night of the fashion show.

By the time November came, Adam had already graduated from the on-site portion of his recovery program and moved back to his house in Beverly Hills, which I knew he no longer took for granted.

Solva's fall fashion show took place in the same beautiful L.A. theater they had used for decades, and while Adam, our friends, and family members waited in the audience, Bristol and I stood near our ready models backstage. That night, I wore a royal blue, knee-length lace dress with a halter top, and Bristol had chosen a teal v-neck jumpsuit that delightfully complimented her natural red hair.

"This is the *best* night of my life," Bristol gushed, her eyes lively. "I can't believe my dress is leading the show! What if someone from Valentino wants to hire me?"

I smiled, sighing heavily as if in a dream.

"I know! Imagine who we could meet at the after party—our whole careers could change tonight!"

"I'm planning on it! But don't think I've forgotten about your mystery man. I still want to meet him tonight if he really exists."

Bristol placed her hands on her hips and raised a brow at me, but I laughed.

"He does *exist* and I promise you'll meet him," I replied excitedly. "I'm sorry I haven't told you anything about him yet... but he's not who you'd expect."

"We'll see about that!" Bristol said, rolling her eyes. "You're such a good girl, Anna—I don't think I've corrupted you at all! Just promise me that he's not boring or sheltered."

Despite my effort, I couldn't hold back my ear-to-ear grin.

"I'll let you be the judge, Bristol."

When the stage manager announced the two-minute mark a moment later, Bristol and I quickly checked our models before we walked further backstage to a large flat screen. We waited in anticipation with other designers for the show to begin, and when the music started in the audience room, Bristol's Dawn Frost was the first dress to glide elegantly down the runway. Many members of the crowd clapped quietly as her dress slipped past them and the model turned right, striding toward a door that would lead her backstage again out of sight.

I could hardly breathe when the Sapphire Nova appeared in front of the hundreds of attendees a few dresses later. The model walked effortlessly as the dress flowed naturally around her, and the ceiling spotlights created a wonderful, glowing sheen across the fabric. I studied the audience's reaction as the model turned left to disappear behind another door that led backstage, and I frowned a little as their praise seemed more reserved than it was for the Dawn Frost. But as more dresses walked the runway, I started to feel slightly better when other designers received the same level of ovation.

When the show ended a half hour later, Bristol and I stood in a line with the other designers in front of the reception hall in a different part of the building to greet and talk to guests. The VIP attendees arrived first, and after Bristol and I received a few business cards from executives, I suddenly heard her gasp.

"I can't believe it," she said in a hushed tone. "Adam Avery is here! You know who he is, right? He's *so* hot."

I said nothing as I smiled almost painfully, and when Adam reached us, Bristol's face turned red while she shook his hand.

"It's a dream to meet you," she gushed. "I'm a huge fan and I can't believe what you've been through recently."

"Nice to meet you," he replied. "My girlfriend has told me a lot about you."

Bristol furrowed her brow in confusion, and before she could reply, I touched her arm.

"What do you think of my mystery man?" I asked happily. "He's not boring or sheltered, is he?"

Bristol's mouth fell open, and she gasped as she glanced at me, then Adam.

"No—this is a joke—you're not *serious*—"

Adam stepped toward me, and as we planned earlier, he dipped me toward the floor while we kissed. My fingers curled around the lapels of his black suit once we stood straight again, and I looked at Bristol, whose face was overcome with all kinds of emotion.

"I guess the secret is out now," I told her. "Adam Avery has a girlfriend, and it's *me!*"

A surprised sound escaped her throat before she finally managed to recover.

"I need to go talk with the executives," she said quickly. "We'll talk later."

Bristol turned and disappeared inside the reception hall, and I grinned as I met Adam's gaze.

"I don't think she'll ever underestimate me again," I remarked, satisfied.

"Probably not. You definitely hit the jackpot."

I laughed and rolled my eyes playfully.

"Ready to have dinner with my parents and meet fashion executives?" I asked pleasantly.

"Of course. Let's go in."

I pressed my lips against his for a few long seconds, and Adam's arm wrapped around my waist as we entered the reception hall.

* * * * * *

When the after-party ended at nine o'clock, Adam and I said goodbye to my parents, who had flown into town a few days earlier to visit and see the fashion show. Afterward, Adam led me outside the front of the building, where I noticed a white limo casually parked along the street amidst all the busy traffic. The driver stood waiting by the back door to the private cabin, his gaze resting on us expectantly.

"What's going on?" I asked curiously. "Is that limo...?"

"Yeah, it's for us," he replied with a smile. "I wanted to do a few special things on your big night."

"A few? There's more?"

"A whole lot more, but first…"

Adam took my hand and led me toward the limo while the driver held open the door for us. I smiled at the middle-aged man before I climbed into the empty cabin, which had an entirely black interior that reminded me of the limo we'd used seven years ago for prom night. I settled into the long bench seat across the left side of the compartment and studied the small bar, mini-fridge, and white wicker basket full of chocolates and exotic snacks on the other side. When Adam sat beside me a few seconds later, he pulled the champagne bottle from the ice bucket and removed the gold foil around the top, then the cork.

I thought he would pour some for us in two wine glasses, but instead, he put the rim of the bottle to his lips.

"Adam! You can't do that!"

"Why not? Everything here belongs to us—take a sip."

I raised a brow as he pushed the bottle into my hands, and as the limo started to move, I took a few sips of the sweet, bubbly champagne, which we ended up passing back and forth.

"Where are we going?" I asked. "I can only imagine what else is up your sleeve."

"Think lights and water," he replied at length. "But you'll see soon. It's not far."

I sighed dramatically, but we shared the champagne and talked until the limo started slowing down less than ten minutes later. Through the tinted windows, I could only make out bright lights against the black sky, but after we climbed out, I realized they were the elevated dock lights of a marina. And in front of us a short distance away, a large sailboat with many beautiful, glowing string lights caught my eye as it floated motionlessly in the water next to a wooden dock.

"Adam…"

"I think a private sail along the coast would be incredible, don't you?"

"Yes! I can't believe…"

I didn't bother to finish my sentence as Adam took my hand again and led me toward the beautiful boat, carrying with him the champagne bottle and basket of snacks. The captain greeted us when we reached it, and after he helped us board, I followed Adam to the wide, flat deck where a blanket was spread out close to the bow. We sat down with the basket and champagne between us, and I stared in wonder at the string lights that surrounded us.

"Is this perfect?" I heard Adam ask quietly.

"Yes. I've never been on a sailboat, or thought of sailing at night in this way. It's like heaven."

"Good, that's what I hoped."

"I can't believe you did all this because of my fashion show. I would say I love you a hundred times, but you already know it."

"I didn't do this just because of your achievement," he said gently. "I also did it because… I wanted to find out if you'd marry me."

I lost my breath as I stared into Adam's eyes, unable to speak or think as I waited to wake up from a magnificent dream that had fooled me. But nothing about my reality changed as Adam reached into his pocket, taking out a small, red velvet box. When he opened it, my eyes fell on a light pink diamond in a halo of small white diamonds, all of which were set upon a rose-gold ring.

"So, Anna, before we set sail... will you be my wife?"

My mouth moved in an attempt to say yes—but I had to breathe to make the word come out.

"Yes—*yes!*—I will be your wife, Adam. Forever."

He grinned as he took the ring from the velvet box and lifted my hand, sliding it over the appropriate finger. I stared at the gleaming diamond for a long minute—marveling at its beauty, and wondering how Adam had managed to make such an excellent choice. Although I had started to believe this moment would come after I became his girlfriend in the hospital, I genuinely had no idea of when to expect it—but Adam had managed to get away with the grand proposal easily because of his timing.

"What kind of stone is this?" I asked. "It's extraordinary."

"It's a peach sapphire. When I saw it... I couldn't get you out of my head."

I sighed with delight and leaned toward him, placing my lips near his ear.

"Before we set sail... I do have one condition for marrying you."

Adam raised a brow, his prideful expression fading a little while I smiled cleverly.

"On the night of our wedding... you must make love to me until dawn."

BLURRED, the sequel to Lucid

Adam and Anna's romance continues as they explore
their new marriage alongside Anna's evolving career in
fashion and Adam's clash with the mega tour.

Find out more at erikaharken.com
and join her newsletter.

About the Author

Erika Harken is an American author who enjoys writing flawed and courageous characters across fantasy, romance, and thrillers. She thought about giving up on writing until she had the idea for Lucid, and her dreams have been coming true ever since.